PASSAGES

THE KINGS OF GUARDIAN BOOK THIRTEEN

KRIS MICHAELS

WWW.KRISMICHAELSAUTHOR.COM

Patriarch & Matriarch of the Marshall-King Family:

Frank Marshall is the widowed father of Victoria and Keelee Marshall. Amanda King is the widowed mother of Joseph, Justin, Jasmine, Jade, Jason, Jewell, Jared and Jacob King. She and Frank are now married to each other. She is now Amanda King-Marshall.

Marshall & King Children

Jacob King is married to Victoria (Marshall) King. They have four sons, Talon, Trace, Tanner, and the baby, Tristan.

Joseph King is married to Ember (Harris) King. They have one son, Blake King.

Doctor Adam Cassidy is married to Keelee (Marshall) Cassidy. They have one daughter, Elizabeth (Lizzy) Cassidy.

Jason King is married to Faith (Collins) King. They have two sons, Reece and Royce King.

Jared King is married to Christian (Koehler) King. They have one son, Marcus.

Jasmine King is married to Chad Nelson. They have one daughter, Chloe Nelson.

Jewell King is married to Zane Reynolds.

Jade King is married with Nicolas DeMarco.

Justin King is married to Danielle (Dani) Grant.

Drake (Simmons) Marshall, is married to Doctor Jillian (Law) Marshall.

Dixon (Simmons) Marshall is married to Joy (Moriah) Marshall.

Mike White Cloud (Chief) is married to Tatyana (Taty) Petrov.

Kaeden Lang (Anubis) is married to Sky Meyers-Lang. They have a daughter, Kadey Lang.

Isaac Cooper (Asp) is involved with Lyric Gadson.

Ryan Wolf (Lycos) is married to Bethanie Clark. They have one son, Ethan. (Dixon and Drake's half-brother.)

The founder of "Guardian" and boss of most of the people mentioned above:

Gabriel Alexander (David Xavier) is married to Anna. They have four children, Gabrielle (Gabrielle

Jacqueline), the oldest daughter, twin sons Deacon and Ronan (David Ronan), and Charlotte (Charlotte Jacqueline).

Happy Reading!
Kris

Joy Marshall sat back in the deep cushions of the leather sofa at the Marshall Ranch. The fact that it was December and damn close to Christmas was blatantly obvious. She leaned slightly to her right and whispered, "Does this shit happen all the time?"

Tatyana's head rolled toward her and shrugged her good shoulder. "During the holidays, yes. Thanksgiving wasn't as bad, but... You'll get used to it. Family, you know."

Joy rolled her eyes. She wasn't actually part of the family. Dixon and Drake Simmons had been adopted by Frank Marshall. They'd changed their last name to Marshall this year, and who could blame them? Their biological father, the bastard, was dead. Thank God. Dixon had asked her to change her name with him. Like she cared? What was in a name anyway? Nothing. She changed names like most people changed clothes. Names weren't important. The person behind the name, that was important.

Her attention switched from person to person, assessing the consequences of the mayhem visited upon the huge living area of the Marshall ranch house. A cyclone of human disorder erupted in spectacular fashion. An array of boxes scattered haphazardly across the great room. Children darted between adults. Strings of lights draped between pairs of grown-ups. Laughter echoed as they attempted to untangle the mess of wires. Others unpacked garlands or set up nativity scenes, while a handful unpacked ornaments and hunted for missing wire hooks to hang the beautiful blown glass orbs.

A box of tinsel erupted, sending the silver strands fluttering to the floor. With squeals of delight, at least six children scurried to the mess and grabbed at the shiny strips. One girl wore a handful as a wig. No, make that two girls. Several boys flung it into the air and danced under it as it fell. Parents sidestepped the miniature humans and attempted to make order out of chaos. *Good luck.*

Tucked in the corner, she and Tatyana melded into the shadows of the room, practically invisible, which suited her. She relaxed into the warm leather seat and watched the loud, boisterous crowd. Laughter, goodhearted ribbing, and tight family bonds seem to permeate the mass of people and pandemonium of strewn... *stuff. Wow.*

Last year, her Christmas with Dixon had been

vastly different. The anemic tree she had purchased on Christmas Eve seemed like a lifetime ago. The sad excuse for a twig she'd purchased paled in comparison to the twenty-five-foot evergreen currently under siege. But that damn twig and strand of lights with the dollar store star represented her rebirth. That scrawny piece of kindling? Best fucking Christmas tree in the history of Christmas.

So much had changed in three hundred sixty some odd days. Last year she had been a different person. *This year?* Well, change was good. *Sometimes. Mostly.* Hell, that was her story and she'd stick to it until someone blasted her fucking happy bubble to smithereens.

"Huh." Sensory overload didn't come close to describing the pandemonium she witnessed.

Tatyana chuckled, but didn't reply. She and Taty had formed a tight relationship. Well, tight-*ish*. Joy recognized Taty as a kindred soul. The ever-present reserved expression in Tatyana's eyes was eerily familiar because it was reflected back in her mirror every morning.

They'd both seen things, and done things, that most people couldn't imagine or understand. She didn't know the specifics of Tatyana's past. Then again, she didn't need to know and would never ask. Tatyana extended her the same courtesy. It was just nice to be able to sit quietly in the company of someone who had walked some of the same tainted paths she'd traversed.

Traversed? No. Still traveled. As a Shadow, she still provided her services to Guardian. However, she was more selective in how she carried out those missions. She no longer put herself at risk unless it was absolutely necessary. She had a husband she loved, a safe home, and although nobody in her previous life would have believed it, friends. She even had a fucking dog that liked her.

Several people she'd never seen before moved through the crowd. Which was plausible. During the last year, assignments for Guardian had consumed several months. Her work, and travelling to Arizona with Dixon, Drake, and Jillian, had kept her away from the Marshall ranch. Plus, she wasn't exactly social. Her eyes tracked the unknown people as they mingled with the crowd.

"That one, the one holding the star, who is she?" Joy motioned with her chin to the woman who'd been fishing in a box for quite some time. She straightened, smiled and handed off the tree topper to one of the King brothers. She hadn't been introduced to him, but he was a King. Family resemblance ran strong.

"Her name is Danielle; she goes by Dani. She and Justin were married this June in Tuscany. You were... away."

"Huh." Yeah, all of June had been taken up on a mission. The longest single stretch she'd been away from the ranch this year. Dixon stayed at the ranch while everyone else traveled overseas for that wedding. He'd said he didn't want to go if she wasn't with him. She gave a mental shrug. Her husband was sentimental like that. Besides, it wasn't like she didn't hear about the wedding. Jillian had reported every detail. Twice. She rolled her shoulders, trying to dislodge tension that resided between her shoulder blades.

The Tuscany wedding must have been... crowded. It didn't really bother her that she missed the gathering. *That many people... This* many people made her itch. However, she'd promised to love, honor, and cherish. Her eyes found Dixon, who suddenly darted after one of the older boys. The child's shriek of laughter turned everyone's heads. She watched as her man scooped up the boy and hung him upside down, tickling his belly. He would make a fantastic father someday. Now if *she* could just figure out how the hell to be a mother. She could do it. Dinner on the table and baths before bed. If she put her mind to it, she could decipher that shit. *Probably. Maybe. Fuck...*

"Justin is the one with the restaurants." Tatyana tacked on.

She nodded. Yes, she'd heard the man was a business genius. He was also a stealthy motherfucker if the rumors were correct. *Information extraction specialist, indeed.* A thief by any other name is a still a thief. The man moved with presence, not as overtly dangerous as the others, but still, if she'd seen him on an assignment, he would trip her instincts as one who bore watching.

She again scanned the people in the room. While a smile didn't visibly form, a bubble of happiness appeared inside her and had taken up permanent residence. Anubis and Asp had found a home. Kaeden and Isaac. She reminded herself yet again of the name change. A group of men laughed along with Chief. Tatyana's man was the overall director of Guardian's complex. Chief's eyes sought the darker corner where they sat. The endearing smile shared between Chief and Tatyana reinforced her opinion of the man. She liked Chief. His approach to communication mimicked hers. Talking just to talk wasted breath. She liked that he got it.

Her newly-minted father-in-law was the best, though. She could sit with him for hours and just... be. She glanced at Frank Marshall. He'd lost some weight and wore his hair in a buzz cut now, but all-in-all he looked good. Strong. Thank goodness. Losing him would decimate this family. Frank and Amanda acted as the foundation that supported the melded families.

Her eyes stopped at Fury. Alive, with a family. The concept was foreign and, for some reason, her brain couldn't connect those two dots. Not the fact that Fury had magically lived through that shit show in Mexico, but that he had a family. Yeah... no. *Fury + family. Does not compute.*

One of the smaller children let out a frustrated wail, and her attention turned toward Faith, Archangel's wife. She oozed maternal charm as she picked her baby son, Royce, out of the portable crib tucked in the opposite corner of the massive room. Archangel, her boss, assessed the situation before he continued his conversation with his brother Jared and Jared's husband, Christian. A special memory involving those two brought a shadow of a smile to her lips.

A young boy started doing summersaults, which resulted in a host of legs, arms, tumbles, and kids shouting for parents to "look".

"How many children do you think are in this house at this moment?" She'd tried to count, but the constant movement made it difficult and rather scary. She liked kids. Even wanted one, someday. *One* being the operative word.

Tatyana chuckled. "It's easy to do the math. I'll list them; you count."

She chuckled, "I had to ask, didn't I?" But she seriously wanted to know, because trying to count the little buggers was like trying to corral cats while a rabid Doberman chased them across a waxed floor. That shit wasn't going to happen

"Yes, yes, you did. So, to begin. Jacob's kids are Talon, Trace, Tanner, and Tristen. Jason and Faith have Reece and now Royce. Jared and Christian's son, Marcus, is probably asleep upstairs. Keelee and Doc have Elizabeth. Kaeden and Skye's little girl is Kadey. Jasmine and Chad have Chloe. Joseph and Ember's son, Blake, is over there. So, what is that? Ten or Eleven?"

"Eleven." Joy surveyed the room again. *Yeah, no.* She watched Jacob make his way through the crowd. Why was he wearing an oversized sweater? She glanced at the fireplace, which stretched across almost the entire back wall of the ranch house. It was warm in the house. Borderline tropical. Her eyes zeroed in on a slight bulge under his right arm. It was the wrong shape for a weapon, but he was hiding something. Not very well, but...

Tatyana nudged her and nodded at Jacob. Yes, she and Taty had similar backgrounds. Moments like these validated that fact. They both tracked the big man and noticed when he caught Doc's attention. Doc gave a subtle nod and bent back down to the ornament box. He placed the glass ball he'd extracted back in its cushioned container. Several minutes later, he slipped quietly through the crowd, and out of the room, following Jacob.

Joy evaluated the scene. Fury, Anubis, ASP, and the crazy one, Jade, all noticed their departure. Archangel did too. None followed. *She* wanted to follow the men. The urge to trail them and find a place in the shadows to learn what was happening danced like ants on her skin.

She glanced at Tatyana. The woman's mouth ticked up in a tiny smile. Ahh... it would seem Taty wanted to know what was going on, too. "Any ideas?"

"Something to do with presents, I assume. This family goes overboard. Last year there was a surprise wedding. We weren't here, but I heard it was quite the event." Tatyana's eyes skimmed the crowd as she spoke.

"Ah, yeah... there were several surprise weddings in the last year." Joy gulped, hard, and admitted, "I've never exchanged gifts for Christmas." *Stalk and kill a monster. No problem. Learn to be sociable? Working on it. Figure out family and the maternal thing? Meh... she was trying. But Christmas presents? Oh, fuck, no.* What if she blew it? What if Dixon didn't like what she'd done? She rolled her shoulders again. Seriously, when had she become *that* woman? The little wifey who worried about Christmas presents and another's reaction to stupid emotional overtures. Her eyes traveled to her husband. A slow smile spread across her face. She knew exactly where and when she became *that* woman. About a week after she'd been assigned to watch over him. An assassin acting as a guardian angel. Instead, Dixon had saved her.

"Chief and I exchange one small gift on Christmas Eve. I've never celebrated the holiday. Before he joined Guardian, he hadn't either. The team he was part of exchanged a gift at Christmas. He said it was usually something like good whiskey. We agreed if we ever have a family, we would expand our tradition, but a simple gift, given from the heart, is enough for us. Of course, I bought a present for Frank and Amanda. They are Mike's family."

Joy nodded in agreement. Frank had officially adopted Dixon and Drake. Frank and Mike had a special relationship, too, although the dynamics were a bit different. Thank-fucking-fully Dixon had taken the gift buying lead for Frank and Amanda. Hell, she could have done up one beauty of a care package. Throwing stars, knives, a vial of poison—you know, simple things from the heart. Yeah, that would have gone over well. Or not. Fuck, she had no clue, so when Jillian had come to her with an idea, she jumped on it. She hoped like hell the whole... thing... didn't backfire. There was a very real possibility of a massive back draft, but it was too late now. The wheels were in motion. Literally.

Stacks of brightly wrapped gifts already sat along the far wall of the room out of the way of the controlled chaos. This family really got into the Santa mode. Amanda, Jasmine, and Jewell entered carrying trays laden with Christmas goodies. Jasmine effectively led the small horde of children to a low table erected for the holiday. It was remarkable how well behaved those kids acted. Talon and Reese, the oldest of the gaggle, took charge of the younger children, marshaling them onto pillows scattered around the table. Jasmine ensured everyone had a cookie, sippy cup, or drink. It took a special person to be able to wrangle that many kids. She made a mental note to scrutinize Jasmine and Miss Amanda when they were around the children. Reconnaissance was key if she wanted to figure the parental thing out. She surveilled the room. Tori and her sister would be other legitimate sources of information. The effortless way they handled all of the demands, questions, and needs of the little humans was amazing. The crazy one? No need to observe her. That sister, well, she understood and sympathized with that one, immediately. Jade was more like her then the other women. One on one, they could handle a kid... for the most part. More than that, and they both looked for a parental unit. One kid, that was cool, almost manageable. Two? That stretched her nerves way too tight. Recognition of her limitations... it was a thing.

Dixon and Chief sauntered over to their corner, each holding two cups. Ah, the spiked hot cider. She'd heard about the beverage and was looking forward to trying it. She smiled and let her eyes appreciate her husband. She liked the way Quick Draw moved. He'd worked his way up to a nine on her sex scale last night. He was inventive, and wow, did he have stamina–she'd give him that.

She accepted the steaming mug and a kiss before she glanced at the door from which Jacob and Adam had left.

"What are you doing?" Dixon sat down beside her and pulled her into his side.

"Watching."

"Anything in particular?" He turned his head to scope out the angle of her stare.

"Jacob and Adam."

"Oh. Why?"

She sipped the steaming cup of spiced, and obviously spiked, cider. "Damn, that's good."

"Yep. Why?" Dixon popped the question again.

She recited the peculiarities, "Bulky sweater, bulge under his right arm. Not a conventional weapon, more of a box shape."

Dixon took a sip of his cider. "Huh. Probably trying to sneak Tori's present upstairs."

"Told you." Taty whispered.

"That hallway leads to the kitchen, Frank's den, and a back stairway to the upstairs." Dixon tipped his head toward the door she was watching.

She gazed up toward the second story. If she wanted privacy, she'd hit up a bedroom upstairs, especially with everyone preoccupied down here. What she wouldn't give to be a fly on the wall.

"Those two men are up to something." She sipped some more of her cider. Damn, she was getting the 411 on this shit. It was good.

"Of that, there is no doubt." Dixon pulled her into his side and kissed her forehead.

CHAPTER 2

Jacob pushed open the bedroom door. A night light flooded the darkened room with a soft hue. The crib that sat in the corner was definitely occupied. He glanced over the railing. Little Marcus was sound asleep. The baby monitor beside the crib was active and listening. He glanced back and out the hallway. Tori and Keelee wouldn't come into this room unless Marcus fussed and his dads didn't answer his cries. It was the safest place he could think of to do this. He tiptoed across the plush carpet and turned off the baby monitor. Hopefully, Jared and Christian would be distracted enough with the pandemonium downstairs they wouldn't notice the monitor being off for a few moments.

He lifted his sweater, careful not to lose the precious cargo hidden underneath. He carefully and quietly placed the small wooden box on top of the dresser where the baby monitor sat. He was excited to show Doc. Hell, he was excited to see what was inside. In order to open the box, Justin had had to special order tools from somewhere in Asia. Justin could have forced the latch, but he'd asked Justin not to damage the box in any way. The small chest had belonged to Keelee and Tori's mother. Justin had opened it this morning when he and Jillian arrived. Keeping it away from Tori since then had been a fucking carnival shell game. The door pushed open. Jacob, expecting Doc, chuckled when Jared peered into the baby's room. "Damn it man, that didn't take you long," Jacob whispered.

"What in the hell are you doing in here?" Jared hissed before he peeked over the crib railing at his son. He crept to stand beside Jacob.

"I'm meeting Doc in here. It's the furthest away from Tori and my room, so I'm hoping like hell she won't track me down." Jacob glanced at the door again. "Did you see Doc when you came up?"

"No, I came up because Marcus has been sleeping for a while. Christian is making him a bottle." Jared glanced at his son again.

Jacob couldn't miss the pride and love in his brother's expression. He knew that feeling. The enormity of caring for someone who is completely helpless and utterly dependent on you changes a man. Marcus was Jared's biological son. Christian would be the donor for the next child. Their surrogate had already agreed to carry their second child. He was damn glad for his brother. The man deserved every happiness in the world.

The door creaked open again. Both he and Jared turned. Doc peaked in and then shuffled in the room, shutting the door behind him. He edged up to where Jacob and Jared were standing. "Is that it?"

"Yeah, I picked it up from Justin this morning. Dude, you have to hide this thing for me. Tori almost discovered it twice today. She knows I'm hiding something. Thank God, she hasn't found me out yet. It has been almost a year since I took this box. She asked about it a couple months ago. I told her it was destroyed when it was opened, and there was nothing in the box." Jacob sighed. He'd hated lying to Tori, but this was one Christmas where the woman wouldn't know what she was getting from him. Well, his and Doc's present. They were going to give it to both Tori and Keelee at the same time. Before he did that, he'd make damn sure the box contained no unpleasant surprises.

"Have you opened it yet?" Adam looked at the box as if it was going to bite him.

Fuck. Jacob so hoped it wasn't going to bite them in the ass. He didn't have another "major" gift to give her.

"No. I needed five minutes to myself to do that. I have four boys, a wife who is hell-bent on finding this without knowing exactly what she's looking for, and a house full of brothers, sisters, nephews, and nieces. When would I have time to do anything by myself?" Jacob rubbed the back of his neck. Today had been nonstop.

This year, the entire family had gathered at the ranch for Christmas without protest. Everyone went out of their way to ensure they were here, together. Frank Marshall had been battling Non-Hodgkin's lymphoma for almost the entire year. His treatments had taken a lot out of the man, but he was one tough son of a bitch. He still worked the ranch and was involved in the day-to-day activities. Frank Marshall had become a father to the King clan and he'd done it without trying to take Chance King's place. Those shoes, nobody could fill. Good thing Frank didn't wear shoes. He wore boots.

"Well, are you going to open it?" Jared whispered. Jacob pointed at the door. "You're the lookout."

Jared reared back. "No way, this is my kid's room. I want to see what's in the box."

"Fine, but if Tori or Keelee walk through that door and see this before we get it wrapped, *you* will be the sacrificial lamb," Jacob growled.

"The only person coming through that door anytime soon is Christian. So, get a move on, little man," Jared whispered and then glanced quickly at the cradle. Marcus squirmed and made a squeaking noise. Jared reached over and rubbed the baby's tummy, settling him quickly.

Jacob took a deep breath and glanced at Doc. "Ready?"

Doc nodded. "Let's do this."

Jacob lifted the tiny latch and pulled the top of the box open. In the glow of the baby's night light, three sets of eyes studied the contents of the box. It had been over twenty years since the inside had been examined. Jacob stared at the contents as a smile spread across his face. Photographs, macaroni necklaces, and pieces of jewelry filled a red velvet tray. He lifted the small stack of Polaroid photos. Pictures of Tori and Keelee riding horses with their mother. The women were duplicates of their mom. There were pictures of birthdays, Christmases, and what had to be Easter, because damned if that wasn't a young Frank wearing bunny rabbit ears.

"This is fucking perfect." Doc lifted one of the macaroni necklaces. The pasta had been dyed. Red and green. Definitely a child's work. Tori had several of the same types of treasures from their boys. Every preschool in the nation must make macaroni necklaces for Mother's Day. Jacob chuckled as he picked up the second one.

Jared pointed to a small velvet tab at the bottom of the box. "Is that for decoration or do you think the bottom comes up?"

Jacob brought the box closer to the nightlight and examined the bottom. He handed Doc the assortment of jewelry and gently pulled the little piece of fabric. The bottom of the box lifted away to reveal a tray holding three envelopes. He handed Jared the velvet covered cardboard and picked up the envelopes. All three men stared as he carded the envelopes out in a fan. One each, labeled, Tori, Keelee, and Frank. *Holy shit*. His eyes had to be the size of saucers. "This could be really good, or really, really bad." His gut was firmly on the side of 'this is bad.'

"Why would there be three letters?" Doc set the jewelry down on top of the dresser. "I mean, I understand if you are deploying, or you know that you're ill and don't have long to live. I get why you'd write a letter to your family for those reasons, but, Skipper, she wasn't sick. She unexpectedly died falling from a horse." Doc gazed at Jacob and then regarded Jared.

"They're sealed. We can't open them." Jacob turned the envelopes and ran his hands over the sealed edge of each.

"So, do we give the envelopes to them? I mean as a Christmas present?" Doc shook his head. "What if what is in those envelopes isn't a Christmas thing? What if what's in those envelopes isn't something family needs or wants to hear."

Jared cleared his throat. "I'm going to take Marcus to Christian. This suddenly got way too personal. Whatever you decide to do, I wish you luck." He reached over and scooped up his sleeping son.

Jacob nodded. He waited until Jared left the room before he turned to Doc. "Chances are the letters are a good thing. Something they'd want to hear."

"Are you willing to gamble this Christmas, which could be our last Christmas with Frank, on that assumption?" Doc took the envelopes and returned them to the box. He laid the red velvet cardboard bottom over them and the red velvet tray on top of that. "Doc… do you really think this is our last Christmas with Frank?" A chill ran down his spine. He'd never asked that question. Honestly, he didn't want to know the answer. It wasn't like him to stick his head into the sand and hope the storm blew over, but damn it, this time he'd done exactly that. He believed Tori had done it too. Neither had acknowledged the elephant in the room, and as far as her father's health was concerned, they pretended life was going to go on without changing. Tori talked to Frank almost daily. She knew about his treatments and told Jacob all the details when they were alone in bed. He'd held her when she cried, and he'd comforted his mother the times he'd come home during the year. But damn it, he'd avoided asking his best friend the hard questions.

"Frank has the best doctors money can buy. Gabriel ensured his treatment is supervised by the best. The treatments are going well, and he's holding up, but we are talking about cancer. As far as I know, it has not metastasized, which is promising. The cure rate on this type of cancer is close to the ninetieth percentile. But, given even the slimmest odds, do you want to take a chance on those letters being bad memories?"

Jacob glanced at the top of the dresser to ensure they hadn't forgotten anything before he shut the lid of the box and fastened the tiny latch. His hand ran over the smooth wood and shook his head. "We should give it to the girls before Christmas."

"That's fine by me. I was able to get Keelee a new saddle and bridle, hand tooled by one of the best leather artists in the nation." Doc chuckled and shook his head. "I can see by the expression on your face you don't have another gift for Tori, do you?"

"I have several gifts, but I was banking on this being the special one." Jacob rubbed his face in aggravation. He glanced at the date on his watch. He still had four days. He had access to aircraft. If need be, he'd pay Guardian for the fuel, pilots, wear-and-tear on the aircraft, and take it on a shopping spree. He'd be damned if Tori wouldn't have the best gift he could give her. Fuck him. He'd hoped the box would have been it.

"There's still time." Doc tapped small box. "If we give them the box tomorrow and preface it by saying the box is a Christmas gift, if necessary, we could still bust ass and find Tori a gift. But if I were you, I'd start a search now. Think about it. Have you ever known anyone to leave letters like this unless they were heading to war or dying?"

"No, and it's killing me not to open that letter. I don't want to give her something that's going to upset her, but this… this isn't our call, Doc. The girls need to make the decision. Open the letters or don't." Jacob put both hands in his pockets and stared at the box.

"That still leaves a question, when do we deliver

that letter to Frank?" Doc mimicked his actions and shoved his hands in his pockets.

"I think we should let the girls determine that." Jacob looked at his best friend. The thrill of giving Keelee and Tori a once-in-a-lifetime gift had come crashing down. The unknown nature of those envelopes? That definitely killed the fun. He shrugged. What could he do? Nothing. "So, can you hide this until we can get the girls together tomorrow and give it to them?" Jacob nodded to the little box.

Doc grabbed it off the dresser. "Yeah, come to the hospital with me. I'll lock it in one of the vacant offices. We can take the girls to the clinic tomorrow. There are no patients. We'll have privacy there."

Jacob nodded. "Sounds like a plan." He followed Doc out the door. Damn it, what the hell was he going to get Tori? He usually planned her gifts far in advance so they were special. Well, this Christmas would be special all right. He just didn't know if that was a good special or an "Oh shit, Jacob, you just fucked up," special.

CHAPTER 3

J oseph barked out a laugh at the small triage area. LED Christmas lights were wrapped around every possible surface. Red and green garlands draped across the door and strands dangled from the exposed beams in the ceiling. "It looks like the Grinch threw up Whoville in here."

"Shut up. Lizzy and Kadey did it." Doc threw a wadded-up clump of garland at him.

"Oh, then it is beautiful," he deadpanned and rolled his eyes.

"Damn straight, motherfucker. My girl has taste." Adam dropped the duffle he carried on an exam table. A clank of glass made everyone cringe.

"Don't fucking hurt the liquor, Doc." Jacob reprimanded.

"Why don't you make yourself useful and go get the rest of the stuff off the porch?" Doc tipped his head at Jason. "He'll need some help."

"What the fuck do you have out there?" Chief busied himself helping Joseph and Adam remove bottles of scotch and bubble wrapped glasses from the duffle on the exam table.

"Dude, over the years I've learned I do not depend on anyone else for this gig." He waved his hand around the triage area.

"Holy shit, there is enough food in here to feed an army." Jason, Dixon, Drake and Jacob entered, each carrying a bag or a box.

"Or, conversely there is enough food in there to feed all the King brothers and the now defunct Alpha Team." Adam shoved the last of the bubble wrap into his duffle and tossed it into the corner.

"Who are you calling defunct?" Dixon piped up.

"Oh, shit. Here we go." Joseph poured himself a damn big portion of scotch and grabbed one of the comfortable desk chairs.

"Defunct? We aren't defunct. We are... shit... we are defunct. Nonfunctioning." Drake blinked up from the bag at his brother.

"Discontinued, superseded," Dixon added.

"Out of commission." Chief handed a glass of scotch to Doc.

"Antiquated," Drake agreed.

"Bull-fucking-shit." Jacob laughed and shook his head. "We are more valuable now, as separate entities, than we ever were as Alpha Team."

"True that. Except him. He has always been worth

his weight in gold. Fucking King Midas over there." Joseph pointed at Justin as he and Nic walked in with Jared and Christian.

"What? What the fuck did I do?"

"How many restaurants do you own now?" Jared unzipped his coat and handed a thermos to Jason. "Unleaded and there is some soda sitting out on the porch. Wasn't sure if Doc had room in here to keep it cold."

"Thanks. You have seventeen now, right?" Jason took the huge thermos and unscrewed the top as he glanced at Justin.

"Eighteen. Dani and I just opened one in Paris." Justin shrugged out of his cashmere overcoat and draped it over an unused table.

"And yet you still steal shit." Joseph stirred the pot.

Justin waited for the laughter to subside before he grabbed one of the glasses filled with scotch and said succinctly, "I am not a thief. I'm an information–"

"–extraction specialist." Every man in the room finished for him.

"Exactly." He smiled and lifted his eyebrows a couple times.

"To being defunct." Joseph lifted his glass. A round of here-here's were followed by lingering silence.

"Who would have imagined this seven years ago?" Christian's soft rumble turned every head.

"Not me." Joseph would never have imagined the twists and turns his life had taken. He glanced around the room. Each face was a study of concentration. Memories, events, struggles, triumphs, hell even failures, had formed each of them but had also welded the individual men sitting in this room into a formidable foundation of the world's largest security company.

"Four boys." Jacob chuckled. "I love being a dad." There was a round of agreement from the men who had started a family.

"I'm good with being an uncle. I can't see us having kids." Nic lifted his tumbler and downed it as everyone laughed. Jade as a mom.

God, Joseph prayed he'd see that day. As much as the woman denied any maternal instinct, he had a feeling she'd rock the mom gig.

"Someday." Drake smiled and shrugged. "Maybe."

"What about you?" Joseph asked Dixon. The fact he'd roped that hellcat of a Shadow was impressive. That woman had sharp as fuck claws. Moriah being all… domesticated. That shit did not add up in his books. But, hey, whatever.

Dixon shook his head. "We've had that talk. Joy wants kids someday, and I'm okay with that. Until then I'll be one hell of an uncle to all your kids."

"We're waiting a couple years. We want to find our normal before we have kids." Justin laughed and shook his head. "Whatever normal is." That statement earned a round of "Amens".

"Chief, what about you and Taty?" Jacob lobbed

the question across the room to where Chief sat beside Jason.

"We might not be able to have any. Been trying for a while. No luck." He lifted his eyes and stared at each one of the men in the room in succession. "We are never bringing that up in mixed company. Taty would be devastated."

"It'll happen someday. Then you can join the diaper brigade." Christian winked at Chief.

"Oh, my God. The first time I changed a loaded diaper... I thought I'd puke." An exaggerated shiver shook Jacob.

"And what is with the color? Why is baby poop *that* color? I thought for sure Marcus was dying." Jared's eyelids peeled back as he spoke.

Christian leaned into his husband laughing. "No shit. He woke the doctor up and demanded a video chat. Of course, he held up the diaper as evidence."

"No, he didn't..." Justin looked at his brother in disbelief.

"Yep. The load slid off as Jared was ranting to the doctor about Marcus needing to be admitted. The entire diaper plopped right onto his bare foot." Christian was laughing so hard tears were forming in his eyes.

"Oh, I can do you one better! Reece had the flu. Faith had an appointment and the nanny was on vacation. That means, I'm home with my son, who is sicker than a dog. Kid swears he's feeling better, so I let him eat some of my sandwich. We're doing great, right? So, we head into the den and I put him in the chair with me. I tell him to be really quiet so I can talk to Gabriel on video chat. Just random shit I need to get off the docket, nothing Reese can't hear, right?"

Doc started laughing so hard he had to set his drink down. "No, don't tell me. Projectile vomiting."

"Both of us." Jason admitted. "I threw up as soon as that smell hit my nose. Needless to say, I needed a new keyboard... desk blotter... pens..."

"Holy shit!" Jacob leaned so far over he fell off his chair, which set everyone off on a new round of hysteria.

Joseph emptied his glass and went back to the exam table for a refill. "What about putting them to sleep?"

"Ninety-nine bottles of beer on the wall." Jacob nodded. "I've passed around a million bottles of beer between the four boys."

"The ants go marching two-by-two." Jason shook his head. "Royce will not fall asleep to any other song.

"Hush little baby." Jared and Christian answered at the same time.

"What about you?" Chief asked him.

"Me? Hell, I just recite the Marines' field manual for breaking down and reassembling the M4. Bores the hell out of everyone." Which was the truth and really didn't deserve the laughter the comment received.

"Shit continues to change." Drake lifted his glass. "A toast, gentleman. To what we were, what we are, and what is yet to be. Warriors, friends, and family, by genetics or by the grace of God. May we live a life that makes this world a better place."

CHAPTER 4

Tori looked at Jacob and narrowed her eyes. "What are you up to?"

Her husband had been in an exceptionally good mood yesterday. Now he acted as if his best friend had died. Her eyes cut to Adam. *Best friend alive and well, so not that.* Doc looked like he'd been kicked in the balls, too.

Jacob glanced around and shrugged. "Babe, please, can we just go? We need to meet Keelee at the clinic." Jacob gave Doc a look Tori couldn't decipher.

"I'm not sure whether to be worried or not." She grabbed a coat from the hook by the kitchen door. She glanced back at the empty room, suddenly not sure if she wanted to leave.

Jacob took her hand and squeezed gently. "I'm really hoping there is nothing to worry about, but my gut tells me you might not like the surprise I got you for Christmas." He lifted her hand and kissed the back of it. "I did it with the best of intentions, but we all know what the road to hell is paved with, don't we?"

"Wait, you mean all this is about a Christmas gift?" Her glance danced between Adam and Jacob. They both nodded their heads.

"Keelee should be waiting for us. Let's get going." Doc took off ahead of them, his shoulders hunched under his winter coat.

Tori snuggled next to Jacob. He sheltered her from the strong wind, pulling her into his body and wrapping his arm around her shoulders. They walked in silence for several minutes before she nudged him with her elbow. "You know I'm going to love anything you took the time to get me for Christmas. You get that, right?"

"Yeah, well, I thought I had a winner for sure until Doc and I took a closer look last night." Jacob smiled halfheartedly at her.

"So you and Doc got a present for both Keelee and me?" Tori searched her mind for something both she and her sister would enjoy. They didn't have much in common. Keelee loved all things dealing with the ranch. Tori enjoyed visiting the ranch, but she loved living in Washington D.C., preferred designer clothes, and had a purse collection that would rival any Hollywood diva. She shook her head and then shrugged her shoulders. "I got nothing. I have no idea what you would get both Keelee and me that we would enjoy equally. I'm sure whatever it is, we'll love it."

Jacob helped her over a particularly icy patch of snow and tucked her back under his arm. "Just do me a favor? If this turns out to be something that, in any way, hurts you or Keelee, remember we had the best intentions."

She glanced up. Deep lines etched into his brow. What could they have done?

Jacob helped her up the icy clinic stairs, and with his hand resting at the small of her back, they made their way to Doc's office. She couldn't imagine him doing anything that would hurt her. Rarely had she seen the type of love her husband had for her and for their children. Some women she knew said the magic faded after a few children and a few years. How wrong they were. She and Jacob had date nights, made plans as a couple, and from time to time escaped the insanity of four boys, to reestablish their connection. Sex with Jacob King was phenomenal. Everyday life with Jacob King was even better.

They followed Doc back through the ever-expanding clinic. Well, actually it was a hospital. Doc was the lead physician. He and Ember rotated as primary care physicians. An orthopedic surgeon flew in as needed, as did an anesthesiologist, or any other specialist. Tori had overheard Chief and Gabriel talking about expanding the hospital's capabilities. Jacob explained that with the new complex in

Arizona, they wanted to regionalize specialties. The hospital here in South Dakota would take patients from both training complexes and those who needed specialized care after being injured while on missions. Arizona would be limited to emergency medicine.

Keelee sat with her feet up on her husband's desk reading something on her phone when they opened the door. Keelee smiled. "Hey, so what's so important that I had to drop Lizzy off with Skye? We were just set to make popcorn for tonight. Mom has washed and dried the cranberries. We have a lot of garlands to string."

Tori shook her head and waved a finger between Jacob and Adam. "These two are being mysterious. They say they have a Christmas gift for us."

She blinked between Adam, Jacob, and Tori. "Well, okay?"

Doc cleared his throat. "Stay right here. I'll go get it and be back in a second."

Jacob helped Tori slide off her jacket and then removed his own.

Keelee looked at Jacob. "So, are you going to tell us what you got us?"

Doc's footsteps could be heard coming closer. Jacob glanced down the hall and nodded. "Remember that little keepsake box of your mom's?"

Tori straightened in her chair, immediately alert. "You told me it was destroyed."

"I stretched the truth. Hell, scratch that. I lied. Justin needed specialized tools from a connection he had in Asia. He got them recently and was able to open the box."

Adam walked into the office with the small wooden chest in his hands.

Tori gasped and her eyes filled with tears. She thought she'd lost that portion of her mother forever. "It's here? It wasn't ruined?" She grabbed the box and set it on the desk between her and Keelee, scooting their chairs closer. Jacob stood beside her as Adam moved around the desk to stand beside Keelee.

Keelee reached toward the box, not quite touching. "He opened it? Really?"

Doc nodded. "He did."

She and Keelee huddled together. Keelee flicked the delicate latch and they both placed a hand on the top and opened the box. Tears immediately filled her eyes. She laughed and then cried. She lifted her eyes to Jacob. "How could you think we'd be upset about this?" She removed an old polaroid photograph from the top of the stack.

"Oh my God! Tori, this is my fifth birthday. This is the day Daddy gave me Avalanche." Keelee waived the picture in the air.

Doc chuckled and crouched down beside his wife, looking at the photo she held. "What is an avalanche?"

Keelee laughed. "Not a what, a who. Avalanche was my first horse. I had a Shetland pony before her, but that animal was so mean Daddy bought me a little Welsh mare. She was absolutely beautiful. I had her for almost fifteen years. I outgrew her... God. If I would have continued to ride her, my feet would have skimmed the ground, but she was with me for a long time."

Tears fell down Keelee's cheeks and a radiant smile split her face. Her own tears fell. She picked up another photograph and shook her head. Her fingers traced the image of their mother. She took a shuddering breath and brought her fingers to her mouth. It had been so long since she'd thought of her mom. The photographs of their family from that time were enshrined in a photo album that sat in her father's den. She couldn't remember the last time she'd pulled the book out to look at it. Amanda was her children's grandmother. It almost broke her heart to think the memory of her mother had been so far away.

"She was beautiful. Just like you." Jacob knelt beside her. His arm wrapped around her shoulder, and she leaned into him.

"Why would you think this would upset me?" Tori asked as she picked up a string of macaroni and laughed. She handed the red and green one to Keelee and picked up the purple and yellow one. "I can remember making these. I was so upset that Keelee used both red and green. The teacher said we couldn't use the same colors. And Mom's favorite colors were..."

"Red and green." Keelee finished for her. "What else is in there?" Keelee leaned forward.

Tori picked out a pair of ruby clip-on earrings. "Do you remember these?"

Keelee extended her hand. Tori dropped them into her palm. Her sister pulled her closer and examined them. She shook her head. "No, the only jewelry I remember Mom wearing was her wedding band and sometimes a small cross." She looked back into the box.

Tori lifted the remainder of the photographs out. A solitaire diamond pendant on a gold chain was next. She held it up by the fragile chain and looked at her sister. "I don't remember this one either." She handed it to Keelee.

Keelee held it in her hand and shook her head. "Nope, but then again, we were young when she died."

Tori nodded and pulled out a gold ring, set with rubies. There was a matching necklace, and a pair of clip-on earrings with the same stones. They both examined every piece and laid the photographs out in front of them. The photos resurrected memories long since forgotten. She glanced at Jacob. His brow was furrowed with worry. "I don't see anything here to upset us. Why were you so worried? This is the best Christmas gift you could ever have given us."

"Absolutely the best," Keelee agreed.

As she smiled at her husband, Jacob glanced at Doc. Adam moved closer to Keelee and placed his arm around her shoulders before he nodded his head. Jacob ground his jaw tightly. His facial muscles bunched as he reached forward and moved the small box closer to him. He tipped it and pulled a small satin tab at the bottom of the box. The bottom of the chest lifted out. Jacob sighed and set the container down. Apprehension began to niggle at her, and both she and Keelee leaned forward. She gasped at the same time as Keelee. Inside were three letters.

"Dear God, is that Mom's handwriting?" Keelee's question was a mere whisper of sound in the silent room.

Jacob reached in and pulled out the envelopes. He handed one across the desk to Keelee. When she didn't reach out to accept it, Doc took it from Jacob's hand. Jacob set the envelope with her name in front of her. Tori couldn't do anything except shake her head. How could this be?

Jacob tapped his finger on the desktop indicating the third envelope. "This one is addressed to your father. After you open and read yours, both Doc and I agreed the two of you should decide whether or not to give this to your father."

"This is the reason you're worried." She reached for the aged paper and carefully picked it up. The folded paper inside the envelope was thin, a single sheet of paper if she had to guess. She held it in her hand and traced the seams at the back. Her sister seemed to have difficulty looking at the envelope their mother had left her.

She set the envelope down on the desktop, took a deep breath, and cleared her throat. "The box is

38

something I'll never forget. You've given us a precious piece of our childhood. These wonderful memories have brought our mom back to us and closer to our hearts. That box is the best Christmas gift I've ever received. No matter what's in this envelope, the fact you preserved this box and opened it especially for us is what I'll remember. I love you."

Jacob leaned in, and she placed her hands on his cheeks. She only then registered the fact she was shaking. His morning stubble scratched her palms, and he smiled. He closed the space between them, and Tori fell into a beautiful kiss as she tried to convey the love she held for this man.

She heard Keelee speaking to Adam. Her words weren't distinguishable, but the meaning was obvious. She was thanking her husband in the same way Tori had whispered her thanks to Jacob. When Jacob leaned away, she closed her eyes and let herself believe the words in the envelope would be magical. She turned to her sister. "I'm not ready to open this. You can open yours if you want."

Keelee finally picked up her envelope and shook her head. "I think maybe tonight after Lizzy goes to bed and after a glass of wine, then maybe we can read it in front of the fireplace." Her gaze was on her husband.

Tori knew how Keelee felt. She didn't want to open and read whatever was in this envelope with an audience. She wanted Jacob by her side and no one else. Although, finding time alone at Christmas at the Marshall ranch would be a difficult task.

As if reading her mind, Jacob whispered, "I'll find somewhere for us, somewhere we can be alone. I'll talk to Joseph and see if he can recommend a place. I don't want to bother Chief now that the complex is quiet for the holidays."

Tori nodded and glanced at the envelope addressed to her father. "After we read our letters, Keelee, we need to discuss whether or not to give this to Dad."

Keelee shook her head. "There is no discussion about it, Tori. That letter is addressed to him. It's his. As a matter of fact, I think we should give it to him before we read our letters. Being sick doesn't make him weak. If he treated us the way we are considering treating him, we'd pitch a fit. That letter is Dad's. We give it to him. Now."

"Well, hell, when you put it that way..." Tori's comment released around of laughter. It was the emotional outlet they all needed. She stood up and placed the keepsakes back in the box. "Let's go find Dad."

CHAPTER 5

F rank looked from the envelope on his lap to his daughters. He'd been feeling pretty damn good the last month or so. The treatments were over until the last battery of tests he'd endured determined what course of action was needed. The doctors were hopeful and damn it, so was he. His type of cancer was a sneaky son of a bitch. Started in the lymph nodes. The survival rate was excellent, especially since it had been caught early. If it hadn't been for Amanda, he would have ignored the symptoms and shrugged it off. But his wife was his angel. He didn't deserve a woman like her, but he'd take her. As a matter of fact, he'd taken her for life, and he wasn't about to let his life end any sooner than the good Lord meant. So, he'd been fighting, taking the treatments, and pushing forward. He was beating this son of a bitch disease... but this envelope, hell, it took the wind out of his sails.

"Tell me again where you found this?" Frank nodded toward the envelope.

"Jacob had Justin open up Mama's keepsake box. We found it in the bottom under her jewelry and such." Tori set the little wood box down.

Frank regarded the chest. Elizabeth had guarded that box like a wolverine guarded its den. She said she stored memories. He never had the desire to see what was in it. Figured it was little things from her past. Hell, the box wasn't very big. "What else besides these letters was in it?" He reached over and grabbed Amanda's hand. Her gentle squeeze was reassuring.

Tori smiled and flipped the box open. "Look at these pictures, Daddy. Do you remember this one?" She drew the top picture from the stack and handed it to him. A chuckle built in his chest. Yeah, he remembered that day.

"Are you wearing rabbit ears?" Amanda leaned over and laughed as she asked the question.

"You could have gone another thirty years without bringing this picture around." Frank grunted and shook his head. "Young people do damn fool things. I was young once."

"Wait a second. Did you just call yourself a fool?" Jacob's eyebrows rose and a smile spread across his face.

Frank sent Jacob an 'eat shit and die' glare. His son-in-law's laughter filled the den. Frank leaned back in his chair and crossed his legs. "Boy, I ain't so old that I can't whoop your ass."

Jacob held up his hands in surrender. "Yes, sir. But it's good to know you were a little foolish at least once in your life."

"Son, I cornered the market on foolish, and then I sold that shit, real quick." Frank leaned back in his chair and caressed the back of Amanda's hand with his thumb. He reached out with his free hand and grabbed another photograph.

Amanda leaned over and took one of the photos from the stack. "Girls, your mother was so beautiful. Both of you are the spitting image of her."

Frank looked at his wife and smiled. The woman had a pure heart. There was no jealousy or irritation at the fact his dead wife's possessions had become a present-day Christmas gift. Yeah, he figured he'd won the lottery when he met Amanda King-Marshall. She was a once-in-a-lifetime love. His eyes traveled back to the picture of Elizabeth. He had loved her. Their marriage was good. Elizabeth hated the ranch, but she tried. He hated that she felt confined, so he worked hard to give her things to make her life here easier. The house was among those things. She wasn't country though, and she loved the city and city life.

Comparing Amanda and Elizabeth was like comparing night to day. Not to lessen his love for Elizabeth because when he married her, he did love her. But now? The love he felt for Amanda surpassed any recollection of the love he'd given to Elizabeth. Maybe it was because he was more mature. Maybe it was because they had the shared experiences of raising a family. Who knew?

Frank phased back into the conversation and smiled as Tori and Keelee showed Amanda several more pictures. His eyes traveled back to the envelope and then up to Jacob and Adam. He glanced from son-in-law to son-in-law and then back to the envelope. The men looked concerned. He couldn't blame them. When he served in the military, he had one of these letters. He listened as the women spoke of memories. He leaned forward and looked into the small box. A smile spread over his face as he lifted the silly macaroni necklaces out of the tray. He remembered the day Keelee and Tori brought these pieces home from vacation Bible school. Tori was so put out that Keelee had used both red and green. For the life of him, he had no idea how they determined Elizabeth's favorite colors were red and green. She adored red. Green? Not so much. Couldn't figure out where his daughters got that idea, but there was quite a row about it that day.

Placing the precious keepsakes next to the box, he looked at the jewelry underneath. His fingers traced the ruby-encrusted jewelry and the diamond solitaire necklace. Yes, he remembered these, and those weren't good memories. The man who had given her this jewelry was someone she'd dated before they'd met. Frank took a breath and sat back. Dated? Well, it was a little more than that. Elizabeth had been engaged to this man. He never did ask why they'd broken up. Didn't figure it was his business, especially after Elizabeth agreed to marry him. Thought the guy was water under the bridge. Gone and forgotten. Apparently not.

"Are you going to read your letter now, Daddy? Tori and I are going to wait until things settle down. Maybe tonight."

"I'm not sure if I'll ever open it." He reached over and squeezed Amanda's hand before looking at his daughters. "Would that be okay with you?"

Tori let out a long sigh. "Whatever you want, but I think I will. I just need some privacy and Jacob." She turned to regard her husband.

His gaze questioned Keelee.

"Same here. Whatever you want is fine by me. Part of me wants to rip this open and see what Mom said. Then there's part of me afraid of what's in this letter. I mean, who does that? Who writes letters and leaves them in a keepsake box? Is that kind of... I don't know, maybe fatalistic?"

He shrugged. "There's no telling, but she wrote these letters and put our names on them. That means she intended for us to read them. I may take my time, but sooner or later, I'll be ready to see what Elizabeth had to say." He looked at his daughters. "You need to make that call on your own."

The girls and their husbands said their goodbyes, and Tori took the little box with her. Frank sat with

Amanda, but his mind was lost in memories. Well, in questions, if he was honest.

"Are you all right?" Amanda leaned her head on his shoulder.

He shook his head and listened as a chorus of children's laughter filtered from the front room into the den. The sound made him smile. His grandchildren, he was so damn blessed. Letting this letter get to him? No. He wasn't going to allow it. "That jewelry in the box? I didn't give it to her."

"You didn't?" Amanda turned to face him.

"Nope. That was from her ex-fiancé. She never wore it. The jewelry I gave her was in her big jewelry box."

"Maybe she didn't want you to feel uncomfortable about her keeping it? It was pretty. Maybe she just wanted to keep it because it was expensive?"

"Maybe." But he didn't think so. Seemed like Elizabeth had been keeping the memory of that man as a private thing. That didn't bode well.

"Do you want me to put this away?" Amanda nodded at the envelope.

Frank grunted.

His wife laughed and picked up the yellowed envelope. "I'll take it upstairs and put in our room. It'll be in your bedside drawer. Now come on, Grandpa, you promised to take the boys to the barn."

Amanda stopped at the door and turned with the envelope lifted in her hand. "I know I don't have to say this, but I love you. What's in this letter doesn't matter. Elizabeth gave us two beautiful daughters; I will be forever grateful to her for that. She's a memory of your past, and nothing she says in this letter can hurt me. Nothing she says can change the way those girls love you or my love for you. You are one of the most amazing men I have ever met. Chance King was my children's father. I loved him; you know I did, but I cannot imagine my life without you in it. If I were to find a letter from Chance, I'd feel the same way you feel right now. What we have isn't a cheat on our love for them, and wanting to know what's in this? It's natural. You know that, right?"

Frank stared at the woman in front of him before he nodded once. She smiled, winked and left the den. How the hell that woman could read his mind was beyond him, but she knew what he was thinking. He chuckled and stood. He had five boys who wanted to go see the animals. His city grandchildren loved animals. He had a surprise for each of them *and* their parents this year. His chuckle sounded in the empty room. Chief had helped him ensure no one would be the wiser. His grandkids were going to love him. Their parents? Probably not so much.

He glanced at his watch. He best get after it, otherwise his grandsons would be racing up and down the halls and tearing the house apart, starting at the rafters. He glanced at the wall where Elizabeth's portrait hung. Right beside it was a portrait he'd commissioned of Amanda. She was right. Nothing in that letter would change how he felt about her. His only concern was if that letter was going to change the way he felt about Elizabeth—or perhaps himself.

CHAPTER 6

Jacob knocked on the door to Joseph's house. He knew Ember and Blake were with Jasmine and the rest of the children at her house. Tori, Jewell, Jade, Dani and Jillian were gathered in the kitchen with Keelee. They were prepping for the cookie decorating party while the children were occupied at Jasmine's. With the amount of children at the ranch, the divide and conquer mentality was efficient and necessary. Later, all the children, both big and small, would gather in the kitchen to decorate Christmas cookies. Jacob could remember the fun they'd had as kids in that small Mississippi kitchen.

"What can I do for you, little man?"

Jacob spun on his heel.

Joseph leaned against the side of his house. The man hadn't aged—other than a few more gray hairs at his temples.

"I was wondering if I could borrow a private location. Tori and I need to be alone."

Joseph let out that low evil laugh. "Dude, you'd think after four kids, you'd be adept at finding private time."

"Very funny, asshole. Seriously, I need a place where we can go and not be interrupted. You know that jewelry box I had Justin open? It had letters in it. Letters from her dead mother to her, Keelee and Frank."

Joseph straightened and nodded toward the compound. "You can use the Shadow area. I'll clear it with Kaeden. I don't believe we have any assets in the facility at the moment, but let me check. I was just heading to Frank's house to grab Jason when I saw you coming here. I'll walk back with you."

Jacob fell into step with his brother. "How are things going for you?"

Joseph shrugged. "Life is good."

The good and bad thing about families is that not much slipped by. He looked at his brother. "But?"

Joseph stopped and crossed his arms. "Gabriel has offered the Arizona project to me."

"No shit? As in running it?"

Joseph nodded.

"That is fucking fantastic. What does Ember think about moving?"

"I haven't talked to her about it." Joseph stared down at his snow-covered boots.

"Why the hell not?"

"She's got the hospital here. It's growing, and there is one hell of a lot of work. She enjoys what she does." Joseph shrugged again. "I'm not going to ask her to leave. Figured I'd tell Gabriel when he shows up the day after Christmas. Thanks, but no thanks."

Jacob chuckled. "Not sure that is what I would do."

"What the hell do you mean?" Joseph growled.

"Look, if there's one thing I've learned since being married to Tori, it's don't make decisions for your wife. It *always* backfires. Women will not do what you expect them to do. You make this decision for Ember and you'll never live it down." Jacob rubbed the back of his neck as he looked toward the ranch house. "Maybe allow her to make that decision for herself."

Joseph started toward that ranch house again. "It surprised me when Gabriel approached me. I figured just staying in the shadows, no pun intended, was what he needed me to do. We have four new identity architects trained. I'm not needed for that purpose any longer, although I review every cover. I'm pretty good at finding nicks and dents in covers, but these guys are too damn good to let a hole slide through. I'm getting long in the tooth, though, you know? I figured I was out to pasture for good."

"Who the fuck are you, and what have you done with my brother?" Jacob laughed as he bellowed the question into the South Dakota afternoon.

"Fuck you, man." Joseph pushed him, almost knocking him off his feet.

"Dude, that sounded almost like you were feeling sorry for yourself. Can I help it if I don't recognize that characteristic in my big brother?" Jacob walked a few more steps with his brother before he spoke the truth as he knew it. "I think you'd be the perfect person to bring the Arizona project in line with the vision Gabriel has for it. What we have there is a good beginning. Dixon and Drake have built the infrastructure, and the entire development is off the grid, but there's so much more to be done. It will take a driving force like you to make that place a reality. Gabriel, as always, has a reason for asking you to take the helm. I don't know what the fuck that reason is, but I guarantee it's valid and that you're essential to the equation. Ask Ember. Don't let this chance pass you by." When his brother paused at the path leading up to the ranch house, Jacob paused with him.

Joseph looked up to the sky and followed the flock of snowbirds as they headed toward the barn. "Life is good here, but if I'm honest, I feel stagnant. I figured once I'd retired from the Shadows, I'd just lie low and fade away. But, man, I'm a fucking father and a husband." Joseph turned his eyes to Jacob. "I never thought I'd have this life. I figured I'd die in some foreign hellhole. I want to show Blake I can be something. I want him to be proud of his old man."

"You want this job."

"Yeah. I do."

"Then ask her. If she says no, explain what you want to her. Just don't assume, man. Listen to your little brother, for once." Jacob threw his arm around his brother's shoulders.

Joseph shrugged Jacob's arm off. "Yeah, well, if I do, I'm not telling you."

Jacob laughed and launched up the stairs to the kitchen. "Never entered my head you would. I'm going to grab Tori, and we'll head over to the complex. Give Kaeden a call and clear us in."

Tori gazed down the long underground hallway. She had the necessary clearance to be in this facility, but the fact that she was actually *in* this place, boggled her mind. She'd had no idea it existed. None. She'd visited the ranch during just about every phase of its construction and still been unaware this massive underground structure was being built. A true marvel.

"Here it is." Jacob held her keycard in front of the digital lock. It beeped, and a green light flashed as the deadbolt system disengaged. Jacob pushed the heavy door in. A light automatically turned on inside. He pushed the door wider and allowed Tori in first.

Tori now knew what Kaeden meant when he'd met them at the facility's entrance and told them, "This is the keycard to one of the eight transitory suites we have below. It's yours until you leave. You both have clearance to enter the facility, so I'm not going to play keeper of the keys. Just make sure to give that to Joseph, Isaac, or myself, prior to leaving. Having new keys made sucks."

Tori looked at the spectacular suite. There were curtains on the far wall. A light behind the curtains simulated daylight. There was a small living room, apartment-size kitchen, and a master bedroom suite. A sixty-inch television hung on the wall over an electric fireplace, and the deep jewel-tone rugs on the floor brought warmth to the space. "Wow. This is amazing. Kaeden said there were eight of these down here?"

Jacob nodded and slid the keycard onto the kitchen counter. "When we were down here for Nic's bachelor party, we only saw a portion. There's a common room, several offices, and an area that none of us was cleared to enter. Since your clearance is higher than mine, you could probably find out, but I'd tread lightly. Shadow business isn't something you should stick your nose into without justification."

"Excuse me? Stick my nose in?" She feigned indignation. It was everything she could do not to laugh at the way Jacob snapped his head her direction. Oh hell, he was so going to backpedal hard.

Jacob's hands went up and his eyes expanded to the size of silver dollars. "Babe, that is not what I meant."

Tori laughed and shook her head. "How much shoe leather have you eaten since we've been married? You think you'd get tired of putting your foot in your mouth."

"But, baby, if I stopped screwing up, you'd be worried. Admit it." Jacob wrapped his arms around her and pulled her in for a kiss.

Tori wrapped her arms around Jacob's neck. She leaned into his warmth and ran her hand through his hair as her other arm pulled him down and closer. She chased his tongue, dancing to a tune only they could hear. It was a song they'd memorized and played from the heart.

Jacob pulled away and glanced at the king-sized bed. He turned back to her and waggled his eyebrows. "We have the room. We have no children at the moment. What say we make use of that big, soft bed?"

Tori smiled up at her husband. "I think you have the best ideas, Mr. King."

Jacob jolted, standing straight. "Really?"

"Absolutely. It's been… ages." Tori laughed at the ridiculousness of the statement as she started to unbutton Jacob's shirt. It had been… three days. His hands grabbed hers.

"It has been a while. Between work and the boys and family… Have I been neglecting you?" Jacob's earnest question preceded his tender kiss.

Tori's breath caught in her chest. "No, you haven't neglected me. If anything, you overwhelm me. Never change. Never stop." She stared into his eyes as she spoke. The man she adored was a romantic, and he wined and dined her, sent her flowers and small gifts. She was constantly amazed by the attention he poured on her.

"Regardless, let's take the time to get reacquainted. Let me make love to you. Then, we can read the letter." Jacob lowered his head and sought her lips.

Tori followed his lead. They shuffled from where they stood to the bed. For every piece of clothing Jacob removed, Tori returned the favor. A small game, one they'd started to play years ago, but it teased and tantalized. She shivered as she removed her panties. The full body shudder wasn't caused by the cold; no, it hinged on the thrill of anticipation. Her husband, naked, hard, and standing proud, swiped the comforter to the foot of the bed. Tori slid onto the sheets, as Jacob moved with her, covering her with his body. The hair on his chest tickled her nipples. Sensitive to the stimulation, they hardened as he held himself above her.

"You are so fucking beautiful." Jacob's eyes studied her face as if he'd just seen her for the first time. He lowered to kiss her, deepening, sweeping, and teasing her with just a bit too much, followed by not quite enough. He left her panting and needing more. She spread her legs, cradling his hips with her thighs. The feel of his hard, hot cock against her sex sent another shiver through her body.

He kissed down her neck and swirled his tongue at the dip of her throat. She rocked her hips into him.

The man knew how to excite her. He teased her with barely there kisses, punctuated with long, sucking pulls only to retreat back to the soft teases. Tori threaded her fingers through his hair and tightened her grip. She pulled him up. His cock-sure attitude and happy smile were too much. She laughed, and he pounced, growling as he tickled her.

She pounded on his back, laughing so hard she was shrieking. "Stop!"

Jacob finally listened and rolled them, so she was on top. "I love you." He pushed the mass of blonde curls over her shoulder.

"I love you more." Tori leaned down to him and kissed him before sucking his bottom lip and pulling it. Jacob rolled them again, not breaking her kiss.

She moved, allowing him between her legs. Fun and games were over. As she gazed into her husband's eyes and the absolute truth of his love, the constant in her life, she saw the man whom she'd built her life around, the man who had given her four sons, and the man who was her touchstone. As he entered her, she sighed in contentment. They'd made love so many times, but each time they came together, the connection between them strengthened. Her body reacted to his. Their hearts beat in the same rhythm and their lives became one song. There were dips and crescendos, bridges and refrains, but the music hadn't stopped. Jacob led her through the familiar, yet still exciting, chords of their love song. She shattered under him and barely registered his thunderous growl as he came. As he dropped over her, resting on his elbows to keep from crushing her, she ghosted her hands over his back. They came down together, heart rates slowing and regaining their breath. They kissed and touched, extending the intimacy. Jacob tilted and flopped to his side, pulling her with him.

"We are so getting a room here whenever we come to the ranch." Jacob's voice reverberated through his chest.

Tori raised her hand. "I second that motion."

His laughter bubbled around her. She adored that about him. He was a happy man. It was impossible to take life too seriously when Jacob wanted to play and, thank God, that was most of the time.

She wasn't sure how long they lay in the bed together. There was no rush, the children were taken care of and there were no phones to answer or meetings to rush to. Life had gotten hectic lately. Strange how it took memories from the past to make you look at the present and the future. Tori loved the job she did, but she wasn't the only one doing that job any more. Granted, she was only supposed to be part-time, but she'd been working more and more as the boys got older. Lately, she'd been playing with the idea of quitting. As the children grew, she wanted to do the PTA thing. She wanted to be a classroom mom. She wanted to be at each of the awards assemblies, recitals, plays, sporting events. The Guardian job diverted so much of her attention from her boys.

"Hey, where are you at?" Jacob rubbed her shoulder. "Are you worried about the letter from your mom?"

Tori shook her head. "No, but I've been thinking—"

"Oh shit, that's never good." Jacob's chest moved up and down under her as he tried to suppress a laugh.

Tori lifted and slapped his shoulder, causing him to laugh harder. "No, brat." She took a deep breath and stared at him.

All playfulness drained from his expression. He tucked her hair behind her ears. "What is it?"

"I've been doing a lot of thinking lately. I was wondering how you would feel about me taking a hiatus from Guardian—at least until the boys are older."

Jacob mimicked her position, resting on his elbow as he looked at her. "You know that I would have absolutely no objection to you being a stay-at-home mom. I didn't think that's what you wanted."

Tori shrugged. "It wasn't in the past. I think it may be now. It's just that over the last year, things at work have started to consume more and more time. I think I'll approach Gabriel and ask him for a leave of absence."

Jacob leaned forward and tenderly kissed her lips. "I'll support whatever decision you make. Our boys are well-adjusted, and they know they are loved. If you want this, then I say go for it."

Tori smiled at him and waggled her eyebrows. "Maybe, just maybe, there will be more time for mommy and daddy."

Jacob smiled at her. "I'll take the fringe benefit."

Tori pushed him down to the mattress. "I somehow thought you would." She climbed over him and off the bed, soliciting several sharp groans from a slip and slide with her elbow and one awkwardly placed knee. She moved through the small apartment to the kitchen counter and grabbed the old envelope. Padding back to the bedroom, she gratefully slid in beside Jacob as he held up the covers.

They settled against the pillows and she twirled the envelope in her hand. "Well, I guess there's no time like the present." She opened the envelope and withdrew the paper. With a glance at Jacob and his confirming nod, she unfolded the single sheet of paper and read aloud.

Dearest Victoria,

I asked your father in the letter I wrote him to give this to you when you turned eighteen. I wanted to explain a few things and hopefully help you to understand why I left.

Tori sat up in bed. Jacob lifted right behind her. "What the actual fuck? She was going to leave Dad? Leave us?" She waved the paper at him.

Jacob took the letter from her hand. "Babe, maybe we should wait until your father reads his letter."

"Oh, hell no!" Tori reached for the yellowing

paper. "She was going to leave us. I want to know why."

Jacob held the paper away from her. "Sweetheart, you need to calm down." He lifted his hand and stopped her from the angry retort that formed on her lips. "We'll read it, but you have to remember your mother didn't leave. We don't know why she wrote these letters. It could have been a bad time in her life. She could have written this letter and then decided to try to make it work with your dad. We don't know."

Tori shook her head. "Don't make excuses. She was going to leave us. Jacob, give me the letter." Tori leveled a stare at him.

He handed her the letter and leaned in to kiss her shoulder. "Just remember, babe, nothing in that letter changes a thing about us, your dad or your sister. This letter is a ghost. It only has the power to upset you if you let it."

Tori nodded and settled next to Jacob in the bed. She lifted the paper and continue to read.

When your father and I met, I had recently broken up with my fiancé. His family was wealthy, not unlike your father's, but his wealth came from old money, not land and cattle. The reason we broke up was ridiculous, at least to me. His parents refused to acknowledge me. I came from poverty and had nothing to bring into a marriage. That made me unacceptable in their eyes. Since his inheritance was tied to their permission, he had to abide by his parents' demands. I was heartbroken. Devastated. When your father and I started dating, I was wounded. Your dad was gentle and kind. He helped to repair my heart. He is such a good man.

As you probably know, your father and I were married because I became pregnant with Keelee. I loved your sister from the moment I knew she was in my womb, just as I love you more than you'll ever know. One day, if you have children, perhaps you'll understand that comment. The bond between a mother and a child is irreplaceable. I hope that my leaving won't break that beautiful relationship, although I know your trust in me will be shattered.

I do love your father, but it's a different kind of love than the love I feel for Richard. Frank Marshall is a wonderful man. He is a fantastic father. I will never take that away from him. What he is not, is the love of my life. Your father deserves to be that to some woman.

I'm dying slowly here on the ranch. I can't breathe. I can't live. It is as if my entire life has been placed in a suspension. I reached out to Richard. It was a hard decision, but one I had to make.

Richard asked me to meet him in Denver. His parents have passed away, and he has inherited. I have to take the chance on being with my soul mate. I'm so sorry for leaving you, baby. If I stay here on the ranch, no matter how much I love you and your sister, I will wither away and die.

I think the greatest kindness I can perform is removing myself completely from your life. I plan on keeping in contact with your father. Hopefully, he'll give you this letter and a telephone number where you can reach me. If you choose not to call, I understand. You are in my heart, *and always will be. I pray that you have grown up happy. I know that if I had stayed, my misery would have affected you, your sister, and your father. Please know I am doing what I feel is necessary. I will always love you, my darling Victoria.*

Mom

Tori dropped the letter to her lap and leaned into Jacob. Her soul was bereft. Her mother, a woman she barely remembered, had been preparing to leave them when she'd died. She sat up and turned to Jacob. "Do you think this Richard knew Mom died? Or do you think he assumed she stayed with us instead?"

Jacob blinked at her and shook his head. "I... I wouldn't know."

Tori chewed her bottom lip. "I can find him."

"You have a first name." Jacob sat up and took the letter from her, scanning the contents.

"Dad would know."

"And you're going to ask him, aren't you?" Jacob folded the letter and placed it on the bedside table.

"As soon as I know he's read his letter. Think about it, if this Richard didn't know... can you imagine what he felt when she didn't show up?" Tori's mind raced at the implications.

"Don't you think contacting this man would upset your father?" Jacob pulled her back down with him.

Tori settled against his warm chest and sighed. "I

don't think so. As gruff as Daddy is, he's one of the kindest men I've ever met. Closure for this Richard is something we can give him."

Jacob sighed and wrapped both arms around her. "Just don't push your dad. Let him take his time, and if he doesn't remember this guy's name, promise me you won't push him."

"I won't, but you watch, he'll remember, and he'll tell me." Tori closed her eyes for a second before she shoved the thoughts of her mother and father from her mind. She was alone with her husband with no chance of interruption. There were so many other things to capture her attention.

CHAPTER 7

J oy stood on the porch of their home and stared down the winding drive that led from the county road to the ranch. She'd fucked up. She shouldn't have let Jillian talk her into it. She paced back and forth on the wooden porch. Sasha, her dog, paced along with her.

"Are you going to tell me?" Dixon's voice didn't startle her. She'd heard him come to the door. The telltale sound of the creaky floorboard, three boards in from the front door, indicated she had company.

Joy glanced at him and narrowed her eyes. Was she going to tell him? She gazed down the long, desolate, gravel road again.

"Seriously, what has you so worked up? Have you accepted an assignment? Do you have to go again before Christmas?" Dixon walked out on the porch and wrapped his arms around her. Of necessity, her pacing stopped.

"Hell, no. We talk about my assignments." They had an agreement. She still worked; he still worked. They talked about her assignments—not the particulars—but she didn't just disappear. Communication. It's a thing, or at least for them it was. No matter how sparse that communication was.

"Then what has you so on edge?" Dixon pulled her tight into him.

The warmth of his body inside his open, down-filled coat reached out to her. She may have snuggled deeper into his chest. Okay, she totally did.

He reached down and nudged her chin up, forcing her to meet his gaze. "You know you can tell me anything, right?"

She huffed and shook her head. "I may have done something."

"Something good, or something bad? And if it's bad, do we need a cleanup crew?"

Joy slugged her husband, garnering a well-earned grunt from him. "I cleanup my own messes." She twirled and walked away, casting yet another glance down the access road.

Dixon snickered. He ambled across the wooden porch and pulled her into his arms. "I know you do, babe. It's one of the things I love about you. Care to tell me what terrible thing you think you did?" Dixon started rocking back and forth, and cradled in his arms, she swayed with him.

"I'm worried you won't like your Christmas gift, and that shit pisses me off. Because, hello, it's a fucking gift. I mean, seriously, if you don't like it, it's not like you can fucking give it back." Joy rolled her eyes at the vomit of words falling from her mouth. She was turning into such a... fucking girl.

Dixon chuckled and lowered his lips to her ear. "I told you we didn't have to exchange gifts this year. I know you don't celebrate Christmas. It's not like I'm forcing you to do this. Whatever you got me, send it back."

Her ears told her before her eyes looked to the horizon. A truck bounced down the gravel road heading toward the ranch. She sighed loudly and shook her head. "Can't." This was really going to happen.

Dixon straightened. His eyes had caught the movement, also. "I thought everybody was here." He turned his head and let out a shrill whistle.

She heard Drake's boots against the floorboards as he came to the front door. "What?"

"Did Frank tell you about anyone else coming out? Do we have any deliveries? I know we don't for the complex, but maybe the ranch?" Dixon nodded toward the truck that was still driving down the long road.

She could distinguish the color now. *Blue.* Strange, she'd pegged him for a black truck kinda guy.

"No. I thought all the feed deliveries were done." Drake opened the storm door and stepped outside.

The warmth of the outside heaters they'd installed on the porch kept it comfortable.

"That is not a delivery." She turned around. "Jillian will want to be here." Joy lifted an eyebrow when Drake failed to move. "That would mean you need to get her."

"Yup, bossy, bossy, bossy," Drake drawled as he turned to go back into their home.

"I wouldn't have to be bossy if you listened the first time," Joy grumbled under her breath. She and Drake got along. *Mostly*. Dixon had yet to convince her his brother wasn't a little… slow.

"Who is it?" Dixon still had his arms around her, although he'd stopped rocking. His attention was firmly fixed on the filthy, four-wheel-drive, metallic-blue, truck. The door burst open, and Jillian bounced outside and squealed, "Is that them? Are they here already? They made good time."

"Is that whom? D, do you know what's going on?" Drake asked as he came out of the house and held Jillian's coat out to her.

Dixon snugged Joy closer to him. "No, but I reckon we're about to find out."

Joy leaned back in his arms to look at her husband. "Jillian and I made arrangements to have your little brother and his family come for Christmas." She nodded at the truck. "That would be them."

Dixon tensed behind her. It was a moment of truth. She glanced at Jillian, who hadn't stopped smiling. Obviously, she had no concerns about the gift.

Maybe *she* was so uneasy with the visit because Ethan's new stepfather was her ex-lover. That was one subject she hoped to avoid. *Very awkward.* She didn't do awkward. Hell, she barely did people.

Drake slapped Dixon on the arm. "Holy shit, we get to meet our little brother. This is fucking fantastic!" Drake pulled Jillian toward the steps and waved at the truck to catch the driver's attention.

"You did this for me?" Dixon whispered the words beside her ear.

She nodded. Yeah, she did. "I knew where Ethan was, and who he was with."

"Who was he with?" Dixon stepped beside her and draped his arm over her shoulder, pulling her with him toward the stairs of the porch.

"He and his mother now live with a prior associate of mine." She shrugged as if she hadn't just told Dixon his little brother was living with a Shadow. Yeah, she could pull off the nonchalant shit. Hopefully, Lycos would keep his mouth shut. She rolled her eyes. Ryan was *not* a conversationalist; he'd keep his mouth shut.

Dixon leaned down and kissed her temple. "Thank you. Thank you for making this happen. I should have reached out before. I wanted to, but I didn't know how his mother would respond."

"From what I understand, she's a good woman who was stuck in a very bad place." She could empathize. She prayed that Bethanie and Lycos would finally find the happiness she'd discovered.

The truck pulled to a stop in front of the ranch house. The back door on the passenger side swung open and a gangly young man hopped out of the truck. "Wow! Mom, Dad, look at this! There's cows over there! And horses, look, look! Horses!"

Joy watched as Lycos exited the truck. Time had treated her old lover very well, but it would seem that Bethanie and Ethan had treated him better. There was a relaxed air and a happiness that exuded from the man. His wide smile as he stared at his son was... breathtaking. She couldn't help the answering smile on her face either.

A petite blonde with a riot of curls that actually bounced as she jumped down from the big truck laughed at her son. "Ethan, slow down. Come over here."

She'd met Bethanie in person in New York when they planned her escape. Since then, she'd talked to Bethanie several times while planning the Christmas surprise. Bethanie's primary concern was Ethan. She was not a fan of keeping their arrival secret. Jillian was the one who practically demanded they keep the visit as a Christmas surprise. The only other person who knew the trio was coming was Kaeden. She had to ensure, one, Lycos was welcome as an ex-Shadow, and two, there would be room for the family on the complex side if shit hit the fan and staying at their house was a no-go. Kaeden assured them the family would be welcome, and there was plenty of room.

Lycos waited for Bethanie and Ethan to stand

with him before he met her eyes. Yes, he'd changed. She'd never seen him so settled in his own skin. She stepped forward and did the introduction thing. "Ryan, Bethanie, this is Dixon, my husband, and as you can tell that is Drake, his twin brother, and his wife, Jillian. They are Ethan's older brothers. Dixon, Drake, your brother Ethan."

The boisterous child suddenly became shy and practically hid behind Lycos. "Hi." The kid lifted his hand and waved.

Neither Dixon nor Drake moved. Joy turned to look at her husband. He and Drake had the same expressions on their face. They were lost in a past full of memories. She reached out and touched Dixon's arm. He jumped and glanced at her before a massive smile split his face. He walked down the steps with Drake right beside him, and held out his hand to his younger brother. "It's a pleasure to meet you, Ethan. I'm Dixon, the smarter, better twin."

"Smarter? Better? No way. I'm Drake; you'll like me more."

"More? No way, because I'm going to show Ethan the barn."

Ethan's eyes were as round as pie tins. Bethanie laughed at her son. "Ethan would love to see the animals. He has a wolf at home that is going to miss him dearly."

"Yeah, but Dog is awesome. He can take care of himself, but Dad and I put out food for him just in case. Some days those damn rabbits are hard to find."

"Ethan!" Bethanie's face turned lobster red.

"What? It's true, right, Dad?" Ethan blinked between his parents.

"I believe your mother was reprimanding you for your language, young man." Lycos tussled the kid's hair as he laughed at the face his son made.

"Hey, Jillian, would you please grab our gloves and hats?" Drake smiled as his wife flew into the house at his request.

Lycos turned to Joy. "Thank you again for inviting us. Ethan and Bethanie have been looking forward to meeting their family."

Dixon, Drake, Ethan and Bethanie were laughing and practically talking over one another.

She looked up at the man she once believed she'd loved. Perhaps she had, in a way. "Jillian led the charge on this one." The woman she just mentioned flew out of the house with an arm full of wool and leather. Jillian tossed Joy a jacket on the way down the steps. To say Jillian was excited would be an understatement.

"Dad, are you coming to the barn with us?" Ethan glanced back at Lycos.

"I'll be there in just a minute." Lycos smiled indulgently at the kid. Ethan shouted okay and took off at a jog to catch up with Dixon and Drake. Bethanie smiled at Lycos and fell into step with Jillian. The two women trailed the trio at a much slower pace.

"Being in love looks good on you." Joy turned her

attention from the gaggle of people heading toward the barn to Lycos.

"It's something I didn't believe could happen." His eyes tracked his family.

Joy got it; she knew that feeling. "Anubis has living quarters for you on the complex side if things don't work out here. He also wants to talk to you. He asked that you set aside an hour the day after Christmas."

Lycos slowly turned and focused on her. No, he hadn't lost any of his intensity. Being happy had just masked it. "Why? I'm no longer a Shadow."

"Yeah, I know that. There are baby Shadows in the pipeline, and a few old friends still working. I have no idea why Anubis wants to talk to you." She shrugged. "Not my monkey, not my zoo."

"So, your husband, he's treating you well?" Lycos crossed his arms over his chest and stared at her.

"Why? You going to pretend to get all protective of me?" That thought actually made her chuckle.

Lycos threw back his head and laughed. "Fuck, no. I figure if he's not treating you well he's as good as dead. But, it would really suck if Ethan's brother ended up pushing daisies. You know what I mean?"

She lifted a shoulder. "Meh, he has his days, but that man, he's fucking perfect for me."

"I can tell. You're looking good, Miho." Lycos dropped his arm around her shoulder. "So, lead me to the barn. I have a feeling before this trip is over, Ethan will be asking for cows and horses."

"Well, it's not like you don't have enough room on that mountaintop." She shrugged into her coat as they walked.

"A mountaintop isn't a place to raise horses or cows."

"One could say that a mountaintop isn't a place to raise a family, period, but you made it work." She bumped into him with her shoulder.

"Does your husband know about us?"

"No. Bethanie?"

"She does, but she knows it's over. Are you going to tell him?"

She shook her head. "We've agreed that our past stays in our past. Keeps the demons at bay."

Lycos stopped at the barn door and stared into the vast South Dakota sky. "I expect someday our demons and our actions will come back to haunt us."

She snorted. "I'll just fuck those demons up so bad they'll whimper and hide in the closet again. You can't let the past interfere with the present or the future."

"Who said the past can't come back to become our future?" Ryan leaned against the barn door, and a smile spread across his face as he watched Ethan stroking the nose of one of the many horses hanging its head over the stall doors.

"I do. Our past is dead. Gone. Especially yours." She nodded toward the people huddled around Ethan. "That's your future."

Lycos shifted his gaze toward her.

She saw the hesitancy to accept the goodness fate had placed in his path. They moved into the barn, toward their family. A mental smile burst across her thoughts. Lycos would get there. He'd figure out this life was permanent. She recognized the look he'd given her. The one that said he was afraid to believe all of this was real. Well, she'd blazed through that hesitancy because she'd felt what he must be feeling. Lived with it. When your life changes radically, catching up with 'normal' isn't easy. Especially for the likes of them.

CHAPTER 8

Keelee held her mother's letter in one hand and a glass of Chardonnay clenched in the other. It had been a long time since she'd needed liquid courage. She stared at her mom's writing on the front of the envelope. It was fluid and graceful and beautiful. Just like her mom had been. Keelee remembered her mom, probably better than Tori did. Her mom was a girl's girl. She could remember her mom painting her fingernails, and she never went outside without her makeup on or her hair fixed. Getting dirty was always met with disdain. Her eyes rose to the fireplace in front of her. Why would she recall that? She chuckled to herself. Who was she kidding? She remembered it because when she was little, she was always dirty. God, she was such a tomboy and a daddy's girl. She was sure she was somewhat of a disappointment to her mother.

One thing she remembered clearly was her mother wasn't a happy person. She racked her mind desperately to recall why she knew that, but she couldn't put a finger on it. It was just a sense, a child's impression. Perhaps it was fabricated or had been augmented in time. Her father had never spoken a bad word about their mom.

She raised her thumbnail to her mouth and chewed on it. For the longest time, she thought her father would never marry again. Hell, he didn't leave the ranch. Who was he going to fall in love with?

Amanda was remarkable. She'd accepted Keelee and Tori as one of her own without trying to replace anything that reminded the family of their mom. Her dad had chosen well.

Adam padded into the living room. His stocking clad feet made little noise on the hardwood floor. "She's asleep. It wasn't a struggle tonight; Jasmine and Chad wore all the kids out. I think two or three were asleep before the trucks made it back from their ranch." He stopped by the small bar and poured himself a whiskey before he sat down beside her. "She loves playing with her cousins."

She settled against Adam's chest. His hand carded through her hair, and she leaned into his caress.

"You don't have to read this." Adam tapped the envelope in her hand.

She shrugged. "I know. I just can't help feeling like a piece of me is suddenly missing. Whatever is in this envelope is either going to fit that missing piece or make that damn hole bigger. I feel... removed? It's almost like I'm talking about someone else." She shook her head before she glanced at her husband.

Adam leaned in and kissed her cheek. "Whenever you're ready."

She handed him her wine glass to hold. She carefully tore the side of the envelope after shaking the paper inside away from the edge. With care, she slid the single sheet of paper out, unfolded it, and began to read out loud.

My dearest Keelee,

You're receiving this letter a little later than I would have chosen to deliver it to you. But I couldn't in good conscience give you your letter any earlier than I did Victoria. She will be eighteen now and able to make her own decisions, which makes you almost twenty. I would wager almost anything that you are a fine rancher and a dedicated, loving daughter. You adore the ranch, the animals, and everything outdoors. We had so little in common. I'm laughing at a particular memory. I wish I could have enjoyed making those mud pies with you, my sweet baby girl.

Keelee teared up at the memory. She smiled at Adam. "I poured an entire bucket of water in the dirt in the middle of the corral and made stacks of mud pies. I was so proud of my 'cooking'. I ran to the house, through the kitchen, and upstairs in search of Mom to show her. The look on her face was one I'll never forget. She was mortified. She changed my bathwater four times. I was a prune by the time she deemed me clean."

Keelee returned to the letter and found her place again.

First, let me say that I love you. I have always loved and will always love you. The unhappiness I know you sensed in me has nothing to do with you or your sister. Before I met your father, I was engaged. For a multitude of reasons, his parents forbade the union. We broke up and that's when I met your father. His kindness and gentle nature healed so many of my emotional wounds. I'm sure you've been told by now we had to get married because I became pregnant with you. Your father loves me, and I love him, but my love for him isn't what it should be.

I contacted Richard, my ex-fiancé. Why? Because each day here at the ranch, I die a little bit more. This isolated life isn't for me. I tried. God knows I tried. As fate would have it, Richard's parents have passed away while I've been here on the ranch. He told me he'd been looking for me. He says he loves me, and he still wants a life with me.

Oh, sweet baby, I pray someday you find the kind of love I share with Richard. That's why I left. I wanted a life with a man I love with all my heart, not just a part of it. Your father deserves so much better than a tepid love from a woman who has given her heart to another man.

The kindest thing I can do is remove myself from your lives. I plan on keeping in contact with your father. I'll give him a telephone number for you to contact me. I understand if you choose not to make that call.

Promise me something? Even though I have no right to ask it of you, please baby, don't try to make this better. I know you. You're such a sensitive, sweet girl, and your first thoughts will be to protect your father and sister. Tori is stronger than you realize, and your father is a wonderful man. I wouldn't have left you with him if he wasn't. They can shoulder this. It isn't your responsibility to fix what I've done.

I look forward to talking to you now that you're an adult. Hopefully, you can forgive me for being selfish and looking for my own happiness. Perhaps one day you'll understand what it means to love someone with all your heart.

Mom

Keelee fell back into the couch. She blinked at the letter in her hands. "She wrote these letters because she was leaving us."

Adam's arm went around her shoulder and tucked her closer to him. He didn't say a word. He didn't have to. His presence was enough.

Keelee lifted the letter and read it once again. She didn't feel anything. Why didn't she feel anything? She turned toward Adam. "I should be mad, right?"

"Why?" Adam stroked her cheek with his hand. It was cold from the drink he'd placed on the table.

"She's right, you know? I am worried about what Dad and Tori are feeling right now. I mean I loved my mom, but she's been gone... forever. This letter? It doesn't mean a damn thing. It doesn't change the way I grew up. It will never negate how much love I have for Dad or Tori. If she had lived and I got this when I turned twenty... Yeah, I probably would never have called her. Not because I'm mad, because I'm not, but because she doesn't matter. Does that make me a horrible person?"

"No. What that makes you is a realist. You approach life the way your father taught you. You live in the moment. You enjoy your life. You love unconditionally, and you press forward. There is absolutely nothing wrong with your feelings. You're a beautiful woman—inside and out." Adam leaned over and took her lips with his. He teased her mouth open with his tongue. They parted after several moments. "I love you."

"Yeah?" Keelee teased and wiggled her eyebrows at him. "Lizzy is asleep."

"Oh, Mrs. Cassidy, I like the way you're thinking." Adam stood and extended his hand to her. She grabbed it and let him pull her up. He enveloped her in his embrace.

God, he still made her feel so safe and beautiful.

Her eyes fell on the letter she'd left on the couch. Yes, she'd found the everlasting, soul mate, kind of love. A chord of regret resonated through her. Her mom would have loved Adam and Lizzy, but she never would have met either of them.

CHAPTER 9

Ethan walked along the snow-covered ground with the two men his mother had recently told him they were coming to visit. The road trip from their mountaintop was exciting, until it got boring. His mom and dad had stopped frequently to look at sites and read the signs beside the road. Which was kinda cool, but after a while all the signs sounded the same. When they turned down the gravel road to this ranch, he was so excited and a little scared. There were thousands of cows, and a bunch of horses up by the barn. He saw dogs around the barn too.

That was all cool, but what was *extra* was the fact he got to meet his brothers. Only they were all grown up. He was hoping for someone around his age. Still, they seemed as excited to meet him as he was to meet them. And they were big. Tall like Harvey was. Ethan didn't think about the man as his father anymore. He had a dad. Harvey wasn't that man.

His mom called him over. He wasn't quite sure what to do so he slipped a bit closer to her. His dad was talking to the other woman. A dog walked up to him wagging its bushy tail. He held out his fingers so it could smell him.

"That's Lady, she's my father's dog," one of his brothers said. Ethan wasn't sure whether it was Dixon or Drake.

Ethan stopped and put his hand on the collie's head. She was a beautiful dog. He looked up at both of his brothers and narrowed his eyes. "You don't mean Harvey, do you?"

His brothers looked at each other. One shrugged and the other shoved his hands into his pockets. He glanced at Ethan's mom.

She had a worried look. He hadn't seen that in a while. Ethan crossed his arms over his chest. "Well?"

"Dude, I'm gonna tell it to you straight. Harvey Simmons may have been our biological sperm donor, but he was never a father to us. We were adopted as adults by the man we consider our father, Frank Marshall. You'll meet him soon; this is his ranch. He's one of the best men we've ever met." The guy rubbed the back of his neck. "I'm sorry if that bothers you, but I can't change it."

"My dad is over there." He pointed to Ryan. "Harvey Simmons was an ass– err… jerk, he was evil, and he hurt my mom, although she tried to hide it from me." Ethan stroked the collie's head and shrugged. "He's dead. My mom's happy. I'm happy, and I take it Harvey Simmons being six feet under doesn't bother you too much either."

One of his brothers, the one holding the taller woman's hand chuckled. "You speak your mind, don't you, little guy?"

Ethan narrowed his eyes again and shook his head. "I'm not a little guy, I'm young, yeah, but I'm old enough to know the facts, to make decisions based on those facts, and have an input into my life." He looked up at his mom and smiled. "My dad, Ryan, taught me that. We don't treat people like they're ignorant until they prove themselves ignorant."

"Well, shit, looks like your dad, Ryan, is a straight shooter, too." His brother motioned into the barn. "How about we check out some of the horses? Maybe go for a ride and visit some?"

Ethan spun to look at his mom. "May I, please? I promise to listen and to be careful."

His mom's eyes got big, but she smiled. She was nervous. He could tell by the way she kept glancing at the barn.

"I'll ask Ryan to come with us. I know you're afraid of horses."

"You're afraid of horses?" The lady who was with his brothers and had handed out gloves and hats asked.

"Yeah, I am. The horses in Central Park terrified me. Let's just say I'm glad those animals are behind very large fences here." His mom waved at the wooden fences.

The woman laughed and stuck out her hand. "In case you didn't catch it before, my name is Jillian. I'm married to Drake. I don't care to ride, and I agree, horses are great on that side of the fence. Anything that big, I give a wide berth. When they get ready to go out for a ride, I'll take you up to the big house and introduce you to the rest of the family."

Ethan glanced between the two women. He liked the lady, Jillian, and liked that she was being nice to his mom.

His mother shook hands with her and smiled. He could tell she was grateful to have someone else who didn't like horses. Not that he could figure out why. Horses were awesome. He followed his new brothers into the barn and stopped beside them in front of a stall.

"Have you ever ridden a horse before?" The short brunette standing with his dad kept eyeing this brother, so that made him Dixon.

"No, but I really want to." He reached up slowly and touched the velvet soft nose of the horse hanging his head over the stall door.

"This old girl is the matriarch of the bunch. Her name is Charmin. She's really old. We don't ride her anymore. We just give her a good life, lots of oats and plenty of brushing. The horse next to her is Peaches. She's is a good starter horse, nice and gentle. Would you like to ride her?" His other brother spoke. He guessed it was Drake.

Ethan caught Ryan's attention. "Dad! Dixon and

Drake said they'd take us for a horseback ride. You want to come, right?"

His dad and the other lady walked up to the stall where they'd stopped. His father lifted a hand and stroked the neck of Charmin. "Sure. I'd like to see some of the ranch."

"Yay!" Ethan spun and looked at his brothers. "Can we go now?"

Dixon helped his little brother saddle his horse. The kid was pretty amazing. He wanted to do everything by himself and asked a thousand different questions about each piece of tack they used. It was as if Talon and Reese had morphed into one person. He couldn't wait until Ethan met the rest of the children. Granted, he was a couple years older, but he had a feeling Ethan, Reece and Talon could have some serious fun exploring the ranch. Good thing both of the younger boys knew what they could and couldn't do and were damn good at following the rules. Ethan had a sense of wonder about him that was amazing and sad at the same time. He wondered what his father had done to the kid. He prayed Ethan was spared the torture he and Drake had endured. Harvey was a sick bastard. He glanced at Bethanie. His heart bled for the woman. He was certain she'd lived through hell.

Dixon mounted and glanced at the people in the

barn. Drake, Jillian, Ryan, Bethanie and lastly Joy... each one was a survivor. They'd made it through personal tribulations and were stronger for it. Granted, some had survived things the others would never know or understand, but they were survivors nonetheless.

He watched Ethan's 'father' help him up into the saddle. Dixon had observed Ryan saddle his own horse. He was proficient. Hell, he was very familiar with horses and handled them in a casual, confident manner.

Dixon chuckled at his twin. Drake was beside himself he was so damn happy. Family meant the world to Drake. He was the nurturer of the two of them. Drake and Ethan rode out of the barn. Drake was showing Ethan how to hold his feet, toes on the stirrup bar, so he could kick out if needed. Ethan mimicked Drake, holding the reins in one hand and lowering his hand so as not to pull on his horse's mouth. The kid was sharp. He and Ryan fell in behind them. As expected, Drake veered to the east. That route would take them through the solar and wind farms. A curious mind like Ethan's would eat up the information Drake spouted. Probably with too many big-ass words attached to the explanation, too.

Dixon glanced at Ryan. "Joy said you worked for Guardian."

The man nodded. "Worked, as in past tense."

"Retired at a young age, didn't you?" Dixon chuckled.

Ryan turned in his saddle. He pinned Dixon with a direct glare. "I'd rather retire early, than die alone."

Okaaay. "How long did you say you've known Joy?"

"I didn't say, and I thought you two didn't discuss the past." The man continued to stare straight ahead.

Well, that was a new stream of light on the subject. Joy had told the former Shadow about their relationship. Strange. She hadn't told *him* anything about Ryan, but he could understand why. He didn't know much about the Shadows, and he preferred it that way. Knowing anything about a Shadow was dangerous. Joy's position in the organization was a tightly held secret, even now. He'd do anything to make sure she wasn't compromised. Keeping his wife safe was paramount.

Dixon rested his hand on the saddle horn letting the horse take its head and pick its own path through the frozen pasture. "True. We, emphasis on the W-E, don't talk about our past. However, you're not included in the 'we' of us."

The man laughed. "I can see what attracted her to you. Mental stimulation for her is a type of foreplay. You can keep her on her toes."

Dixon cranked his jaw tight. Ryan knew Joy better than a passing acquaintance. "Obviously you know my wife… well."

The man cast a glance up at the sky and shrugged. "I knew her when she wasn't who she is now. We were *friends* when there was no one else for either of us. Things change. For the better in her case and in mine."

Dixon digested the man's words. Ryan obviously wanted him to know whatever had transpired between him and Joy was over. He glanced at the man next to him. Did he feel threatened by the former Shadow? Was he jealous? Yes, fuck him he was jealous, but that was on him. Joy was brutally honest with him at all times. She would have said if she still … yeah. Not going there. This man was by all accounts in love with Ethan's mom. He needed to swallow his jealousy and move on. And he would. *Maybe. Probably. Eventually.*

Dixon visually swept the land before him. They avoided large drifts of snow and rode a little out of their way to put the horses on clear, level ground. Ethan's laughter put a smile on his face.

"How long have you been out of Guardian?" Dixon nodded toward the boy in front of them. Ethan laughed again and pointed to the first windmill that came into sight.

"Since they came into my life. The decision to leave Guardian behind for them was easy."

"I understand that." And he did. He couldn't imagine his life without Joy. If the only way to keep her was to leave Guardian? He would have done it in a heartbeat. "How bad did Ethan and Bethanie suffer because of our fucking sperm donor?" Dixon knew if anyone would tell him it would be the man beside him.

"I don't know how much you knew about that bastard. Bethanie and Ethan escaped, but they will both carry the mental scars for the rest of their lives. Ethan grew up fast. He missed a lot of his childhood. He's an old soul in a young man's body."

"Harvey was a sick, twisted, son of a bitch. We lived through shit no one should ever be exposed to, and I can only imagine what he put those two through. Is there anything we need to worry about? Triggers or anything that would bring back bad memories?" He didn't want to unintentionally hurt his new family.

Ryan shook his head. "Even after all the crap that man put them through, they are remarkably well-adjusted. Hell, they're better adjusted than I am." The man gave a low, evil laugh.

"Finding it hard to adjust to the light of day?"

Ryan glared at him.

He smiled innocently.

With a long-suffering roll of the eyes, Ryan looked forward again.

"No. I've always tried to live in isolated areas. No desire to live amongst the savages, if you know what I mean. So, we live on the top of the mountain. I worry about Bethanie and Ethan. It's a solitary life, but since the threat against them has been negated, I make it a point to make sure they both get out and experience things."

Dixon glanced over at his riding companion.

"Solitary isn't necessarily a bad thing. How is he going to school?"

"Accelerated classes online. The kid is a genius." The man chuckled.

"What's so funny?"

"I was thinking about Guardian. The shrinks there told me I was a genius. If they ever saw what that kid up there could do? Man, they'd pay for his education in a heartbeat. I just don't know whether or not I want him to be a part of Guardian."

"Why? Do you know something about Guardian that I don't?" Dixon tensed in his saddle. He'd never heard anyone say a bad word about Guardian.

"No, hell, no. You don't understand. This kid? He has brains like I've never seen before, and that's saying something. I've seen a lot of shit. He's destined for great things. I don't know if it will be with Guardian or out there in the world, but mark my words, that kid will make an impact that will reach forward in time."

Dixon nodded. He'd noticed how smart his little brother was just from the limited interaction he'd had with the kid. "If you ever need anything, and I mean anything, reach out to us. Family is everything. We wanted to meet and take care of them when all the shit with Harvey was exploding around us, but their safety was paramount. I was a target, and Drake was officially dead. Technically, both of us are dead at this point, except we've taken different names, and we'll probably never go back to D.C."

"Yeah, how's that working out for you?" The man beside him chuckled as he asked.

"Not bad. Being dead isn't as boring as I thought it would be." Dixon laughed along with Ryan. The guy wasn't bad, little green monsters aside. "Seriously, though, I was going to contact Archangel and request permission to meet after the holidays. The fact that Joy and Jillian brought you here as a Christmas surprise was fortuitous. Drake and I understand all too well what that little boy went through. If he ever needs to talk or work through something that bastard has done to him, we will be there for him."

Ryan held up a gloved finger. "First, a word of warning, never let him hear you call him a little boy. You'll get a lecture."

"Yeah, been there, done that, got the t-shirt." Dixon laughed.

"He's a spitfire, that's for sure. I'd like them to have family they are close to, you know? I never had it. I think it's essential for him, especially. Bethanie and I have talked, and we plan to do our best to make sure we include you in his life." The man leaned forward and twisted at the same time so he could look straight at him. "That being said, if either of you hurt that child or my wife in any way, I will hunt you down and kill you." A cold, deadly stare indicated the former Shadow felt he could carry out his threat.

He twisted in his saddle and regarded Ryan steadily. "And if you hurt that boy or his mother, the

95

wrath of God will seem insignificant compared to what *we* will do to *you*."

A very faint uptick of a smile on the corners of his lips preceded Ryan's nod. "Good to know we're on the same page." The man tickled his horse's ribs and the animal moved into a trot.

"I can see why she loves you," he called.

Ryan leaned forward over the neck of his horse and the animal took off.

He chuckled as he watched the assassin reining in his horse to ride next to his son. He couldn't have picked a better man to take care of his brother.

CHAPTER 10

Frank Marshall placed the receiver of the phone back in its cradle. His hand shook just a bit. Well, that was to be expected. Talking to doctors always sent his nerves a skitter. He wiped the sweat off his brow. Fuck him if his knees weren't as week as a newborn foal's. Maybe he was just a little more nervous than he'd admitted, even to himself. Not telling Amanda about the call today had been hard. He wanted her support, but... it was Christmas. The woman deserved a few days without the constant worry his health inflicted for most of the last year. His mind trudged through all the doctor-speak and the final questions he asked. Translating the words into English, he repeated what the man had said to made sure he understood what the doc was trying to tell him. He took a deep breath placed his hands on his hips and let it slowly escape from his lungs. Well, that was that.

His eyes moved across the room to Amanda's dresser. Her little bits and doodads were held in crystal plates and fancy little China cups. He strolled to the solid wood bureau and ran his finger across the top of her jewelry box. He lifted it and gazed at the contents. She still had the gold badge from when Chance was a sheriff. He lifted it out and examined it. Speaking out loud to ghosts didn't seem completely stupid at this point in his life. Hell, he'd talked to Elizabeth routinely when the girls were growing up. He'd kept her informed about her girls, their trials and triumphs. He eyed the bedside stand where Amanda had placed that envelope. Perhaps today was the day to read it after all. Steps he needed to take brewed in his mind and knowing the score all the way around would be best.

He gazed down at the sheriff's star again. "You have one hell of a family, Chance. I'm proud to be able to care for them. The world is a better place because of them. That don't happen often. I'll keep watch over them as long as I'm able. Until my dying breath." His throat constricted. He cleared it and nodded at the badge. "I promise." He carefully set the badge back in the little jewelry box and ran his fingers over the gold chain and earrings he'd given Amanda for their anniversary. She wore them every evening to dinner. That right there, that was the woman he married. She loved hard, and for that he would be forever thankful.

Frank squared his shoulders, closed the lid to

Amanda's jewelry box, and made the arduously long trek across the master bedroom to his bedside table. Strange how fifteen feet can sometimes seem like fifteen miles. He sat down on the bed and opened the drawer. The sound of children's laughter and conversation drifted through the open bedroom door. He took the envelope out and slid the drawer shut. He looked at Elizabeth's fluid handwriting and smiled. She was a concise lady. Lady being the operative word.

Elizabeth hadn't been a good fit at the ranch. She didn't like the animals, the dirt, the mud, or the isolation, but she'd stuck it out. He wasn't sure she would. Theirs was a relationship of necessity. Oh, he had loved her as much as she'd allowed him to love her. But…

He tapped the contents away from the edge of the envelope and carefully opened it. Before he unfolded the paper that slid out, he closed his eyes and bowed his head, trying to mentally prepare himself for what she'd written. There was nothing she could pen that would change where he was today. His daughters had grown into fine women. They were strong, courageous, wonderful mothers and had husbands who adored them. Nothing Elizabeth could say would change any of that.

"What the fuck are you afraid of, Marshall?" Frank mumbled to himself and shook his head as he flipped the paper open.

Frank,

. . .

I wish there could have been another way to explain what's going on in my life. I love you; you know I do. But we both know the kind of love I feel for you isn't what a wife should feel for a husband. My love stems from my gratitude. You picked me up, reminded me that I was worthy, and you loved me. I wish I could love you the way I know you wanted me to. I will forever regret the fact that I have caused you almost daily pain. No one with a heart as pure as yours should have to suffer through a loveless marriage, and I can tell you're suffering, too.

I contacted Richard about two months ago. His parents died in an airplane crash about the time Keelee was born. He has inherited, and he wants me back. He's been searching for me. He says he's never stopped loving me, and I'm so sorry, but I still love him. I tried; God knows I tried. I wanted so badly to be the wife you deserved and a mother the girls could look up to.

If you're reading this, that means I've gone to Denver to meet Richard. Walking away is impossibly hard, and I've struggled for so long with this decision. Keelee and Tori are your life. I would never take them from you. I only ask that we keep an open line of conversation so that if they ever need me for any reason, you'd be able to contact me. I've left letters for Tori and Keelee. Please wait until Tori is eighteen to give both letters to the girls. I feel, as adults, they will better understand my reasons for leaving.

I don't know how to tell them why I'm leaving. I will let you tell them what you think is best.

I'll call. I don't know when. I imagine you won't want to speak to me for a very long time. Richard will send divorce papers. I asked him to make sure you have sole custody of the girls. I would like visitation rights, but I understand if you refuse.

I wish our story could've ended differently. I wish I could have loved the ranch like Keelee does. I wish I could adore you for the wonderful man you are like Tori does. I wish for a lot of things, Frank. My most fervent wish is that you will forgive me one day. You were my savior when I needed rescuing. Hopefully, you will find love and flourish. Thank you for giving me yourself and our daughters.

Elizabeth

Frank set the paper down on his nightstand. She'd intended to leave. He leaned back on the headboard, suddenly exhausted. Thoughts swirled around his mind like sparrows flitting around the barn in the spring. He'd always known she wasn't happy. He'd seen the brightness fading from her. He figured sooner or later she'd get around to leaving him. It was, he felt, inevitable.

He remembered the morning she died. He'd saddled her horse, and she'd said thank you. He could tell she was sad—always so damn sad. He remembered watching her ride out. The one thing she enjoyed at the ranch was riding her little mare. Elizabeth had been exceptionally quiet for, hell, almost a week, maybe longer. Knowing what he did now, he reckoned she was probably gathering her nerve to drive away. Only, she never came home from that ride. Her horse wandered back to the ranch without her. He and his hands scrambled to find her. They'd found her body about dusk. She'd fallen from her horse and broken her neck. At the time, everyone figured it was just a freak accident. A snake, or something else had spooked the little even-tempered mare. The horse she rode wasn't skittish, never reared or bucked. They couldn't figure out how Elizabeth had lost control. It hadn't been until recently they discovered it was Christian Kohler's father who'd spooked the horse. According to the medical examiner's report, Elizabeth had died instantly. For that small mercy, he'd be eternally grateful.

He shook his head. Elizabeth had deserved better. She'd deserved to live the life she wanted with Richard. He would've let her go. Hell, she'd been so miserable he'd almost suggested it. Hindsight being twenty/twenty, he sure as hell wished he would have, but there was no way to change the past. He closed his eyes and listened to the muted voices traveling up from the living room. The house was alive, full to the brim, and happy. He wished Elizabeth would've known this kind of happiness. He wished she would've been able to meet Richard in Denver.

He needed to round up Tori and Keelee and have

a talk with them. He had no idea what the letters Elizabeth wrote them said. He was certain there would be questions. He'd answer those he could and struggle with the ones he couldn't. He glanced out the window to the hills beyond the barns and meadows. Life had a way of twisting and turning, not necessarily the way people expected either. Well, no sense putting off the inevitable. Frank squared his shoulders and drew a deep breath. He glanced at Amanda's jewelry box. No secrets lay in that box.

He stopped at the door and looked upward. "Elizabeth, you can rest well. I understand."

CHAPTER 11

Dixon headed up the stairway just as Frank was walking down. "Hey, I have somebody I want you to meet."

Frank stopped on the stairs and cocked his head. "Who's that?" He looked around the great room. It was just family.

"Joy and Jillian invited our little brother, Ethan, for Christmas. His mom and stepfather are with him. The guy is ex-Guardian, so he's been checked out. They're good people. They are staying with us, but if it's okay with you, I would love to invite them up here for dinners and Christmas." Dixon shoved his hands into his jean pockets. "I'm heading to Rapid City tomorrow to make sure they have gifts under the tree."

Frank's hand landed on his shoulder with a strong squeeze. "Son, you didn't have to ask. That's your family, and that means they are now *our* family. Bring them to dinner. Tell him we expect them at all meals, and all family events. They'll either get sick of us or love us."

His son's face cracked open wide with a smile. "We just got in from going for a ride. Ethan took to horses like a cat to cream. His father, well, his stepfather, went with us." Dixon glanced around and whispered, "He was in Joseph's line of work."

Frank caught Dixon's eyes and nodded. "Seems to me, he'd be a good protector for the child then."

Dixon smiled. "Yes sir. Ethan's mom is a nice lady. She and Jillian are getting along well. Bethanie, that's her name, does hydroponic farming. I think Jillian has a new hobby brewing. Poor Drake."

Frank chuckled. Drake's wife was in constant go-mode. Her mind absorbed and questioned everything. She was perpetual motion in human form. Unlike Joy. They were as different as night and day, but damn it if they weren't each perfect for his boys.

Dixon turned and walked down the stairs with him, adding, "I saw John Smith on the way up. He wanted me to tell you that the new solar heaters installed on the watering troughs were worth their weight in gold. The old ones were crap."

Frank grunted in agreement.

Dixon chuckled. "Bethanie, Ryan, and Ethan are at our house. I'll bring them up for dinner. I know Ethan, Talon, and Reese will probably hit it off, although Ethan is a couple years older. From what I understand, he didn't have much of a childhood, so any type of fun he could have with the kids would be a good thing."

"I'll stop down and meet them before dinner. Kinda ease them in to the press of people." Frank nodded toward the great room. "Right now, I need to talk to Tori and Keelee. Give me an hour or so and I'll be down."

Dixon's eyes were sharp and worried.

Frank hated that his health issues had caused that immediate response from all his family.

"Is there anything at all that I can do to help?"

He forced a reassuring smile to tip the corners of his mouth. "Not a thing, son. This has to do with their mother. Just something that needs to be done. You get yourself back down to that house and stop worrying about me." He winked at Dixon. "Have you told him how big the family was?"

Dixon chuckled. "Yeah, but they don't have a clue."

He grunted. "They will. Soon."

Frank caught Tori's attention and tipped his chin toward his den. She nodded then and glanced toward Keelee. Frank waited for Tori to look back at him before he inclined his head to include Keelee. He gently extracted himself from his grandchildren, who seemed to swarm around him whenever he was in the house, and headed toward his den. He drew a deep breath, steeling himself for the rest of the day.

His eyes dropped to the small bar. *Why not?* He poured himself a small glass of the good stuff. Waiting to drink the fancy liquor or do the things he'd always put on hold for some time later? That wasn't happening anymore. Time on this earth was too damn short.

Frank sat down in the conversation group and waited for his daughters. They trailed into the office one after the other. Keelee headed straight to the bar. "What do you want, Tori?"

"Give me some of the single malt." Tori sat across from her father.

They waited for Keelee to finish pouring the drinks and sit down.

He leaned forward and steepled his fingers together, choosing his words carefully. "I read the letter your mother left me. Let me preface this by saying she did not tell me what she had written to you. Your mother was very unhappy here at the ranch." He was tentative, not quite sure how much detail he needed to give.

Keelee cleared her throat. "She told me she was leaving us." Keelee glanced at Tori who crossed her legs.

Tori nodded. "Yeah, and why." She kicked her foot in the air quickly and repeatedly.

Oh, his little girl was pissed.

He smiled. "Your mother tried hard to make a go of it here. It just wasn't in her. I watched the life drain from your mom, day by day, little by little. Her leaving to go find happiness, that would've been okay with me. I would've fought like the devil for you girls. She wouldn't have won that battle, but in her letter to me, she told me she wanted me to have custody of you. I would've been fine with joint custody, but she didn't ask for that. You both belonged here on the ranch with me. She knew it."

"How can you be so calm about this?" Tori leaned forward.

Frank took a sip of his scotch. "What could I have changed? I loved her the best way I knew how."

"I still want to be mad at somebody." Tori took a sip of her whiskey. "Maybe I can be mad at Richard." She shrugged. "But part of me wants to find him and tell him what happened to Momma."

Frank leaned back in his chair. He hadn't thought about that. Elizabeth just cutting off all communication, it would've been very difficult for Richard Berkley to understand. "Did she give you contact information for Richard?"

Keelee shook her head. Tori mimicked the action.

Frank closed his eyes. "His name was Richard Berkley. That's all I know, except that his family lived in the Virginia area. His parents were some highfalutin society types." He sighed and opened his eyes again. His daughters' worried expressions pained him.

"That's more than enough for me to find him. My question is, do you care if I do?" Tori swirled her whiskey in her glass, staring at the amber liquid instead of looking at him.

"If you're sure this is something you want to do, I'm fine with it, but I'd like to be there when you talk to him," said Keelee.

He considered what Tori and Keelee had said. "I think Richard Berkley deserves answers, but there's nothing that says he will take a phone call from you." Frank took another sip of his scotch. "But he knows my name, and he'd probably take a call from me."

Both girls leaned forward. Tori stared at him. "Dad, you don't have to do this."

"That is where you are wrong. Doing the right thing? That is always a moral obligation. Your mother loved that man. He needs to know." Frank shrugged. It was cut and dried. He would want to know.

Keelee turned her head and spoke to her sister. "How long will it take you to find him?"

Tori tossed the rest of her whiskey down. "Give me five minutes on a Guardian computer and I can tell you his Social Security number, his suit size, and his credit rating."

Frank chuckled. "His phone number would do."

Tori sniggered. "Yeah, but maybe, just maybe... wouldn't it be cool if he was like four-hundred pounds now?"

Keelee giggled. "Only you would think of something like that."

He took another sip of his scotch. "I'm heading

down to Dixon and Drake's. Their little brother is here. Let's make that call after dinner." He stood and finished his drink.

Tori stood and stepped into his path. "Daddy, you've always been my hero. I don't know why Momma couldn't love you the way you deserved, but I'm so happy you found Amanda. I'm sorry you were alone for so long."

Frank pulled her in for a hug. "I wasn't alone. I had my girls. God saw fit to bring Amanda into my life as my girls were learning to live on their own. What is that saying? When He closes a door, He opens a window? I'm plum happy with the window that opened."

Keelee wrapped her arms around both of them.

He extended his embrace to include his oldest. "You girls are the single most wonderful blessing your mother could have left me. I thank the good Lord every day for both of you."

He heard Keelee's muffled sniffle. "Damn it, Daddy, you're making me cry."

Tori's head nodded up and down, and he heard her sniffle, too. "See, that's what you get when you talk too damn much." He grunted and squeezed his girls tightly. Their laughter was a soothing balm to his soul.

Frank smiled as he walked into the dining room and

viewed his entire family and all their children. Three tables were crammed into a space that could comfortably hold two. The children's table was pushed up against the adult table making a sharp L out into the hallway. It was too noisy, too close for comfort, and absolutely perfect. He pulled his chair back but remained standing at the head of the table. He cleared his throat to speak. It was as if someone had flipped the switch. Everyone stopped talking. *Well, damn, he had the floor now, didn't he?*

"This year has been full of ups and downs for us. Our family has grown. I have new daughters-in-law, new grandsons, and an entirely new branch of our growing family." Frank nodded to Bethanie, Ryan, and Ethan. He grasped Amanda's hand. He couldn't hide the fact he was trembling from her. Her hand squeezed his, and he looked down into her beautiful eyes. He didn't deserve this woman, but he blessed the day God put her in his life.

"Those are some magnificent highs. We had some pretty big lows, too. Thanks to Amanda, I went to the doctor instead of gutting out what I thought was a lingering flu. It turns out that Non-Hodgkin's lymphoma can mask itself like that; but because Amanda asked me to go see a doctor, I did. I was blessed to have access to the best doctors in the world. I owe a debt I can never repay to Gabriel and Anna for almost instantaneous access, which as we all know, isn't the norm. Healthwise, this past year was hard. It made me realize how precious every day with my family is and always will be, and I need to let you all know something. Today, I received a telephone call from the specialist in charge of my care. He told me there was no reason to see me again." He put his hands on his hips and cleared his throat. The emotion rolling through him forced him to take a break. His voice cracked and damn it, he fucking teared up. "It would seem that the treatments have worked."

The dining room erupted. He figured his smile could be seen from outer space. Amanda was in his arms and crying. His family had somehow all gathered around his seat at the table. It took damn near twenty minutes to get everybody settled down again. Maybe he should've thought about telling them after dinner. He chuckled to himself. He hated not eating on time.

CHAPTER 12

Ethan walked quietly over the wooden floors. He slid his feet into his boots and put on a coat. His mom and dad were asleep, but it was Christmas Eve. How could they sleep? He was excited. He'd seen how Dixon and Drake turned on the big outside heaters. They'd showed him what to do. He quietly opened the door. Both the cat and the dog came out with him. He went over, lifted the plastic cover on the switch and put it in the proper position, flicking it to "on". The radiant heaters activated immediately. He walked to one of the swings and sat down. The little fluff ball Joy called a dog bounced in the air trying to get up. He reached down and grabbed the tiny thing and placed it in his lap. The cat, missing part of its ear with a kink in its tail, jumped gracefully onto the seat with them. He held the dog in his lap, and the cat launched to the back of the swing and draped itself over his shoulders. The cat's purr rumbled and squeaked. He smiled at the sound and looked out at the clear, dark, star-strewn sky. It wasn't too dissimilar from the sky at night on their mountaintop.

The door hinges squeaked, and Ethan tensed. Dixon and Drake stepped out onto the porch. "What's the matter, too excited to sleep?" Dixon asked as he sat down on the porch swing with him.

"That, and I was thinking about stuff." He stroked the puffy dog's fur and shrugged.

"What were you thinking about?" Drake asked as he sat down in a chair next to the swing.

"Why was he so damn mean? Why did he hurt my mom? What was he going to do with me when he took me away from her?" Ethan looked up at his brothers. "I know you know."

He watched his brothers as they exchanged looks. Great, they weren't going to talk to him about it, but he wanted to know. He wanted to understand how a man could be so evil. It scared him a little bit to think maybe someday he'd turn out like Harvey, but he couldn't tell his mom that. Just thinking it scared him. How could he be sure he wasn't going to be like his dad?

Dixon leaned forward and clasped his hands together. He chewed on his bottom lip for a moment before he spoke. "We used to ask each other those questions all the time. As a matter of fact, for a long time both of us wondered if we were going to turn out like him. It terrified us. Fortunately, we met some good people, got a damn good education, and went to work for an organization that has high morals and standards. We refused to become what he was. We refused to hurt innocent people; instead, we decided to help those people."

Drake cleared his throat and agreed. "We were lucky in one way. We had each other. You're lucky because you have your mother and Ryan, and now you have us. Even talking about what he did to us used to terrify us. It was almost like if we said something, it would make it happen again." Drake laughed uncomfortably. "Hell, even now, talking about him makes my skin crawl."

"He hurt my mom. Did he hurt your mom, too?" He watched as his brothers looked at each other again. He was starting to understand they could communicate with each other without talking. It must be cool to be that close to someone.

"Our mom was probably the victim of our father, but she hurt us both, almost as much as he did. Our uncle, her brother, took us in. It was the chance we needed. We've learned to take what's given to us and make the best of it. Do no evil." Drake gave him a sad smile.

"Before we met Ryan, Mom was always afraid. Harvey did that to her. I tried to do what he told me to do so he wouldn't take it out on her, but I'm so glad he died. I don't care if that makes me a bad person." He glared at his brothers, challenging them to tell him he was wrong.

Dixon reached over and placed a hand on Ethan's knee. "It doesn't make you a bad person, Ethan. What you need to do now that it's all over is move forward. Finish school, figure out what you want to do with your life, but above all else, whatever you do, leave this world a better place. Your dad said you're kind of a genius."

"Are you kidding me? *He's* the genius. He makes computers that do things I don't think they're supposed to do. Did you know he built our house? It's inside a mountain. The reason I knew all about solar energy is because that's what he uses to power our house. My dad is the best!"

Ethan didn't want his brothers to think their stuff wasn't cool, so he quickly added, "I like the windmill farm. It has practical applications here on the plains. It would be difficult to reinforce the structure on a mountainside. The infrastructure of the necessary cabling would be difficult to deal with in a forested area, don't you think? The footprint would probably be too vast for a vertical terrain." Ethan laughed as a little dog flopped onto his back demanding belly rubs.

"That right there proves your father's point. You, my brother, are very smart. Hey, Jillian is an awesome mechanical engineer. She's got, shit, what is it now, fourteen new patents on solar energy technology. How about after Christmas, you two go to her lab, and she can show you around." Drake smiled at him as he spoke.

"That would be *extra!*"

"Ahh… is that good?" Dixon asked.

"Well, yeah." Didn't these guys speak English? Of course, extra was good. He would love to look at her stuff. He glanced toward the huge house where the massive Christmas tree stood profiled in the bay window. "Are we going to the big house for Christmas in the morning?" Ethan had seen all the packages underneath the tree. He hadn't had a Christmas away from Harvey before. His mom was allowed to get him two gifts each year. His mom had tried to make Christmas special. She'd told him stories about when she was a little girl. He liked those stories. She was happy when she talked about her family. He used to make his mom a Christmas gift every year. He didn't have money and neither did she, but she'd cherished every one of his gifts. She kept them in a little box and that box came with them when they'd moved to the mountain in the middle of the night.

"We are. Is that okay with you?" Dixon glanced at him.

He got the feeling his answer was important, but he didn't know why. "Sure. It's going to suck not having gifts for Talon and Reese." He wished he would've known. His dad would have taken him to the city to go shopping.

Dixon leaned back in the swing and pushed it. The rocking action seemed to make the cat purr louder. "I remember my first Christmas here. It was kind of overwhelming. One thing I've learned about Christmas at the Marshall ranch, Christmas isn't about gifts, although some of the younger kids may argue. Here, Christmas is about family, about growing bonds that last a lifetime, and about making sure everyone knows they are loved."

Ethan glanced at his brothers. He smiled and nodded his head. "I like the sound of that."

Drake stood and stretched. "I don't know about you, but morning is coming awful fast. How about we all hit the hay and see if we can get some sleep. You can take the critters to bed with you. Both Dixon and I would appreciate it."

Ethan stood when Dixon did, sending the swing rocking behind them. He still held the little dog in his arms. The cat leapt gracefully to the floor and wound itself around Drake's legs. He shifted the ball of fur in his arms. "You know, someone needs to tell Joy this isn't really a dog. Sasha's more like, I don't know, maybe a dog-ette."

He wasn't expecting the reaction he got from his brothers. For some reason, what he said made them laugh like loons. His gaze went to the doorway. His dad stood with his arms crossed and a smile on his face. He winked at him and turned away, heading back to bed. He hugged Joy's little dog in his arms. Maybe Dixon and Drake were right. *Do no evil.* He liked those words. They made sense. He could do that.

CHAPTER 13

F rank crossed his ankles as he lay in bed. He listened to the sounds of running water. The evening had been chaotic, wonderful, and filled with family and laughter. Except for the half hour conversation he'd had with Richard Berkley. The girls and Amanda had joined him in the den after dinner. Tori had the telephone number and damn it, his fingers trembled when he punched the numbers on his desk phone and put the call on the external speaker.

"Hello?"

"I'm looking for Richard Berkley. This is Frank Marshall."

"Frank Marshall?" Confusion echoed in the man's question.

"Yeah, I was married to Elizabeth Frazier." He closed his eyes when he heard the man's gasp.

"Was?" Was that hope or perhaps desperation?

"Yes, is this Richard?"

"Yes. I'm Richard. Is Elizabeth..."

"Richard, Elizabeth died in a tragic accident almost twenty years ago. My daughters and I recently found letters from her to us that indicated she had planned on leaving us and coming to you in Denver."

He glanced at Tori and Keelee. The man's weeping threatened to bring tears to everyone in the room. Even him.

"She was going to come to me?" Wonder and desperation filled his question. He could only imagine what the man must have thought all these years.

"Yes, I believe she was, but before she could, she was thrown by a horse and died. Instantly. Had I known anything about your plans together, I would have let you know." Reassuring the man his intentions were pure was important to *him*. He wasn't an asshole. He'd have been hurt, but damn it he wouldn't have withheld this information from Richard.

Silence had reigned at that point, until the man sniffed a bit and asked, "Why are you calling now, after all these years? Not that I don't appreciate it, but what initiated the call?"

"My daughters found a secret compartment in Elizabeth's jewelry chest. It held three letters. I don't know what she said to them, but the letter she wrote me said you were the love of her life and she was leaving me to be with you."

"Oh, God." There were muffled sobs on the other end of the line. He grabbed Amanda's hand, and she squeezed his back. It took a couple of minutes before Richard spoke again. "I never married. I always wondered what happened. Why she didn't..."

"She would have, Richard. Had she lived, she would have."

"Thank you. Thank you for this. I don't know if I would have been as gracious if I were in your shoes."

"Elizabeth wasn't happy here. She loved us, but she was in love with you."

"Thank you. You have no idea how well timed this call was for me." The man cleared his throat and in a stronger voice continued, "I will never forget this kindness. Thank you."

"You are welcome. Live well, Richard."

"I will now. Thank you, Frank."

A click ended the call. It took another thirty minutes before he and the ladies could leave the den and face the joy and happiness in the house. They sat, mostly in quiet, absorbing the way life was and what could have been. Life was like that, wasn't it? Happiness, love and joy were wonderful things, unless they were missing in your life. Moments of knee-bending grief and life-sustaining reparation needed the solace of quiet moments to integrate into the fabric of a soul. Whether that solace belonged to your family or a stranger across the country, the need to give the moment the respect it demanded weighed heavy on him, and he could sense the same feeling in his family.

The en suite bathroom door opened, and Amanda

stood backlit by the soft yellow light of the vanity. "You are the most beautiful woman I have ever seen." Frank lifted the covers as she approached. She slid in next to him, her body soft and warm next to his skin.

Amanda reached up with her fingers and traced his face. "I should be mad at you for not telling me sooner."

"You can be mad at me all you want." Frank lifted to his elbow and looked down at the beautiful woman underneath him.

"I could never stay mad at you."

Amanda gave a little sigh when he leaned down to kiss her. His hand traveled across her skin. She was absolutely flawless. Time had left its stamp on her, that was true. Her hair was more gray than dark brown now. The lines beside her eyes were deeper when she laughed. They got tired faster, but there was still fire burning in both of them. Banked a little by age, sure, but the heat hadn't diminished.

"Well, that's a real good thing, hon. Because you got me for years, and years, and years." Frank punctuated each word with a tender kiss.

"That's the best Christmas gift anyone could give this family." Amanda shifted to allow him to settle between her legs.

"I love you. If it wasn't for you, I wouldn't have gone to the doctor. We wouldn't have the time we have now." Frank wrapped his arms under her shoulders and covered her completely. Gratitude for the new lease on life he'd been given only intensified his need to be with his wife.

Making love at their age took a little more foreplay, a little longer to stoke the fire. He made sure he took care of his woman before he allowed himself to tumble over that blissful cliff. He pulled her close to him, and she rested her head on his shoulder. His hands played in the strands of her hair. He'd never tire of holding this woman.

"Another year passing. They seem to go quicker and quicker as we get older." Amanda tipped her head up and looked at him. "Why do you think that is?"

He grunted. His woman laughed at his response. He drew a deep breath and blew it out before he spoke. "I think once you reach our age, you realize just how valuable each minute is. When you treasure something, you pay attention to it. We watch each minute fly by, knowing the next isn't guaranteed. I reckon that's why they seem like quicksilver. Moments of life flash and shimmer in front of our eyes before they're gone forever."

"You know, for man who speaks as little as you do, your words are very poetic." Amanda rolled slightly and kissed his chest.

He grunted and then laughed as his woman dissolved into giggles.

$\approx$

Ryan eased back into bed and pulled Bethanie close to him.

"Oh, my goodness, you're freezing. What were you doing?" Bethanie curled up next to him and shivered.

"I heard Ethan get up. So, I went to see what was going on." He didn't sleep well in another person's home, even though he did believe the ranch was secure. A lifetime of training had ingrained the need to be on guard.

Bethanie propped up on her elbow and looked down at him. "Is he okay?"

The moonlight that permeated the room provided enough illumination for Ryan to see the concern in her eyes.

"I believe so. He had some questions for his brothers. Questions I'm sure he didn't feel comfortable asking either you or me. Mainly about their father and why he was such an abomination." Ryan accepted Bethanie's weight as she lay down on top of him. He ran his hands through her riotous curls and thought for the millionth time how fucking lucky he was.

"I was hoping they would be able to help him," Bethanie whispered against his chest.

"Joy trusts both of them. Hell, she married one of them. I think we can trust them to answer Ethan's questions. They genuinely seem to care. Christmas should be interesting." The amount of people in that ranch house for dinner was... stifling, although he had seen Anubis, Asp and Bengal. Anubis reminded him he needed an hour before Ryan left. Probably to do an official debrief.

"I wish I would have known. We could have done a little more shopping. I did get presents for Dixon, Drake, Joy and Jillian and Ethan is all set."

Bethanie had already given him his Christmas present. She'd married him this past summer and before they left, she'd presented him with a ring. That fall, she'd sold their excess veggies and canned jams. They made the trip once a month to the city and the farmer's market. She did well and usually sold out of her produce and canned goods. He never asked what she did with the money. It was hers. He thumbed the silver band on his left ring finger. It was simple, sleek and perfect. He liked wearing a symbol of their love. Her ring was similar. He'd surprised her with it at the ceremony. A small silver band. She hadn't wanted a diamond and he'd honored her wishes.

Ryan had been thinking for a while now about what present he wanted to give Bethanie. He'd talked to both Dixon and Drake this afternoon while the women were occupied in the kitchen.

"So, I was wondering, Mrs. Wolf, as my Christmas present to you, would you like to go on a honeymoon?" Her elbows landed on his ribs and he groaned. For being a tiny thing, she could inflict damage.

"Where would we go? What about Ethan's school?

When?" Bethanie fired off the questions one after the other.

"Well, if you'd consider it, I thought we could bring Ethan here and let him get to know his brothers while we fly to Fiji or maybe the Maldives." He held her wide-eyed stare.

She blinked and blinked again. "Oh, I don't know what to think about that."

"About which part?" Ryan laughed underneath her.

"Ummm... All of it? I mean, yes, I think Ethan should come and visit his brothers, but what do his brothers think about that? And then there's the matter of flying. We have to go over water, right? I can't swim. What happens if we need to get back? If Ethan needs me or you? We would be what... how many hours away? How far is Fiji or the Mal...?"

"The Maldives Islands."

"Yeah, that. Can we get there in a day? Can we get back in the day? God, what would Ethan think? Would he think I don't want him with me?" Bethanie stopped and pushed up off his chest, seating herself beside his hip. Palpable worry dripped off her.

He reached out and ran his hand from her shoulder to her fingertips. He laced their hands together and brought the back of hers to his mouth, placing a tender kiss on the delicate skin. "I know the thought of leaving Ethan terrifies you. I'm not asking you to do this tomorrow. We can research every question you just asked. We'll talk to Ethan and make sure he's comfortable staying here. I was thinking maybe next summer. That would give you plenty of time to find out the answers to every one of your questions. But as far as Dixon and Drake? They would love to have Ethan here. They did say they may be traveling to Arizona and should he be here at that time they asked if they could take him with them."

Bethanie slowly bent down and placed a kiss on his lips. "I hope you never get tired of settling my nerves. Someday I won't be afraid of my shadow."

He wrapped his hand around her neck and held her close to his lips. "I will never tire of loving you. I promise to consume you within my protective shadow, one you will never have to fear." Ryan rolled them and deepened their kiss. This woman was his life. Their son was their future.

Keelee flopped into bed, exhausted, both mentally and physically, but the tree at the ranch was now loaded with presents for the children. Dixon had made a last-minute run to Rapid City to buy a few presents for Ethan, and Keelee had volunteered to wrap them for him tonight. She was so damn happy they had finally met their little brother. His mom, Bethanie, was a sweetheart. So damn young and innocent. She could hardly remember being that young.

Adam rolled over and pulled her into the warmth of his arms. His voice was groggy as he snuggled against her back, spooning her. "Well, Mrs. Clause, is everything set for the morning?"

"As set as it can be. I swear Tori had to stand guard outside her boys' rooms. They were so hyped it took forever for them to fall asleep. Reece and Talon are bunking together, so that was a dynamic duo of hilarity. Jade and Nic took Royce for the night, so Jason and Faith had a night alone, which is something I don't think happens often."

Adam jerked his head up. "Jade is watching Royce?"

"No, Jade and *Nic* are watching Royce."

"Oh, must have missed that. The kid's safe, then." Adam snuggled down again. "Lizzy was a wild child until about ten. She faded out on the couch."

"Thank you for distracting her. I'm glad everyone made it this year." Glad and exhausted. She'd worked her ass off so Amanda didn't have to worry about anything.

"I talked to Frank after dinner. The docs are very pleased with his progress. His check up in six months will be a full battery of tests, but as it stands now, they are declaring his treatment a success."

"That cancer has a high cure rate. I looked it up on the internet, but I was still scared shitless. I don't know what I'd do without Dad."

"You'd push forward, the way he taught you."

Adam turned her in his arms. "You're so much more than you give yourself credit for."

Keelee scoffed, "I'm just a rancher."

"You're that, and a wonderful daughter, a fantastic mom, and a sexy as fuck lover." He leaned down and kissed her. "I'm the luckiest man in the world because I get to see all the aspects of you shine every day."

"Every day? Well, Doctor Cassidy, is that your way of saying we need to have sex more often?" Keelee slid her hands up his muscled arms.

"Oh, woman, I wouldn't complain about having sex every day." He lowered and took her lips again.

Keelee's body ignited under his touch. Her body heated and her pajamas were pushed over her head. Adam's lips traveled slowly over her skin, stopping and lingering at the spots that drove her insane with need. She ran her fingers through his hair and clenched them when he tongued her nipple. She arched her back into his caress. His gentle touch and soft kisses had always driven her insane. Her life was hard, rugged, and demanding. Their love was the antithesis of the hardness they lived day to day.

Tears filled her eyes when he entered her. Tears of happiness and of relief. Worry and stress had kept her stoic, but here, with her husband, she could allow herself to be soft, uncertain and afraid.

"It's all right, sweetheart. Everything will be all right. I've got you. Let it go." Adam kissed her neck as he thrust deep inside her.

Keelee arched under him as she allowed herself to do just that. She was safe here in Adam's arms.

~

Joy rolled over when Dixon came back into the room and undressed. "Was the kid okay?" She narrowed her eyes at her husband. "Do not get the idea you're going to put your cold-ass feet on me."

Dixon laughed, jerked the covers off her and jumped into bed, plastering his cold-as-fuck body against hers.

She tucked her knees and pushed him off her with her legs. He laughed and braced himself on his hands in a push up. "I didn't put my feet on you."

"Dick. I didn't pony up for this shit." She opened her legs and he dropped down, settling between them.

"Yeah, my dick was cold too. Admit it, you knew what I was when you married me."

Joy grunted in agreement. Yeah, she did.

"Ethan's fine. He wanted to know about Harvey. We were as honest as we could be." Dixon shrugged and concentrated on playing with a strand of her hair rather than looking at her. She got it. That period in his life was brutal.

"You think that bastard hurt him?" She'd go find the motherfucker's ashes and burn him again. That kid Ethan was all right. Well, as far as kids went, he was, but all kids kinda fell into a wait-and-see category with her. She was just now checked out to handle Talon and Reece. Their parents actually let her watch them for short periods of time. The older boys were talkative and curious, but they listened when she told them something. That was pretty fucking awesome.

"I think Harvey had a mental mind-fuck going on, but talking to Ethan, I don't think it had escalated to the physical abuse—yet. He wasn't old enough. Thank God." Dixon dropped his head to her shoulder.

She traced her fingers up and down his back. The muscles jumped under her touch.

"So, how did I rate on Christmas gifts?" Joy tried to make the question seem casual, but damn it, she wanted to know.

Dixon lifted his head and his eyes traveled over her face almost as if he could search out and find her insecurities. "Bringing them here was probably the best Christmas gift Drake and I have ever been given. Thank you."

Joy pushed his hair back from his forehead. "That isn't all you get for Christmas." She lifted one eyebrow and waited.

"What else did you get me? Gummy Bears?" He hitched his eyebrows up repeatedly. The man-child.

"Nope. Guess again." Joy lifted her hips grinding into his erection. His eyes rolled back in his head.

"Please, for all things merry and bright, tell me we

are going to have mind-blowing sex." Dixon thrust against her hip.

"Just so we're clear, Quick Draw, I only do mind-blowing sex on Christmas." Joy pushed him up onto his knees. His cock was hard and pointing straight at her. She reached over to the nightstand and opened the drawer. Looking back over her shoulder, she pulled out a red satin ribbon, wrapped it around her neck, and tied it in a bow. She turned around and leaned back against the headboard. "Merry Christmas, Dixon. Tonight, we reach ten."

"I retract my earlier statement. *You* are the best present I've ever received." Dixon dropped to his hands to the ribbon and slid it off her neck. "I love you."

CHAPTER 14

"Dix, man, would you hurry up?" Drake whined as he lifted onto his toes and patted around at the back of the kitchen cabinet. *Score*. He pulled the plastic bag forward and a smile split his face. He dropped the five-pound bag of sour gummy worms onto the game board they'd set up on the kitchen table. It landed with a resounding thud, moving all the pieces off their squares.

"Awesome!" Ethan grabbed the bag from the board and reset the game pieces.

Drake snatched the bag, ripped it open, and scattered half of the contents on the tabletop amongst the three of them. "You can't play strategic games like this without sugar reinforcements." He popped a blue and red, sugar-coated worm into his mouth.

Ethan grabbed an orange and yellow one and bit it in half. Speaking around his gummy worm he laughed, "You just want reinforcements because you're losing so bad."

"See, that's just it. It's highly improbable you can anticipate the genius of my moves. My conquest is imminent. Failure to register this tactic would be unpropitious and lead to ominous consequences." Drake leaned forward and stared at his little brother.

Ethan stopped chewing and snorted. He turned to Dixon. "So… why does he use all those multisyllabic words? Is there a problem with his brain?"

Ethan jumped out of his chair and away from Drake. It would've been an effective move had he not been laughing his ass off. Drake grabbed Ethan and, as they fell to the kitchen floor, tickled his ribs until the boy nearly screamed with laughter.

"Stop! Stop! I give. I give. Get off me."

Dixon wiped the tears from his eyes as he reached down and grabbed his twin brother by the belt, hauling him off Ethan. It was all he could do to hang on to Drake who was laughing as hard as Ethan. God, the kid was perfect.

Dixon released Drake and they all ended up on the floor in a pile of laughter. "Ethan, my man, you are one hundred and fifty percent our brother." Dixon reached out his fist. Ethan's smaller knuckles bumped his.

The two men scooted up to sitting, backs braced against the base cabinets.

"Do you always talk that way?" Laughter filled Ethan's voice as he asked Drake the question.

As it fell backwards, his head hit the cabinet with a thunk. "Dude, I don't know how long ago we started doing that shit. I think it was in high school. For comic relief, you know what I mean? But now it's like a habit, and you gotta admit learning new words just to piss off your brother, it's epic."

Dixon's head rolled toward Ethan. "Next time you visit, you can impress us with your vocabulary."

Ethan sat back against the cabinet and mimicked the positions Dixon and Drake were in. He draped his arms over his knees. "I don't know how often we can visit. My mom is still really afraid of everything. I don't think she's gotten over knowing people were trying to kill us. My dad, he makes sure we're safe." The kid stared at his fingers for a moment. "Maybe, if Dad says it's okay, you can come to the mountain. I'd like you to meet Dog, but he's really more wolf than dog."

Dixon shot a glance at Drake. "We'd be honored to come visit you on your dad's mountain. He was talking about taking your mother on a honeymoon someday. We were thinking maybe you could come here and stay with us while they did that."

Ethan blew out a lungful of air. "She won't go. She thinks I'm still a baby, I mean holy crap, I'm going to be driving soon. Dad says her apron strings are really short. Whatever the hell that means." Ethan dropped his legs out in front of him.

"She'll come around, dude. You're lucky to have a mom like her, you realize that, right?" Dixon studied his younger brother. Damn, he could see the resemblance between the three of them—same nose and jawline, same strawberry blonde hair and blue eyes. The kid was going to be as big as they were, too. You could tell by how gangly he was now.

Ethan sighed. "Yeah, I know." He grinned at Drake. "Are you ready to get your ass kicked?"

"I don't believe your mama would appreciate you using those types of words," Frank Marshall drawled as he walked in the kitchen.

Damn, how had he not heard his father come in the house? Oh, right... Mad tickles in the middle of the kitchen floor. He chuckled at the memory.

Ethan scurried to his feet. "No sir, she doesn't."

Dixon reached up and Frank extended his hand, pulling him and then Drake to their feet.

"I came down because Charity is in foal. Seems to me every member of this family has a horse they claim. I figured whatever foal Charity throws should go to the newest member of our family." Frank crossed his arms and looked at Ethan.

Ethan blinked at Frank and his mouth fell open. "Me?" His disbelief was almost comical.

Frank nodded. "Yup. Now I know you wouldn't be here enough to take care of it on a daily basis, but when you are here, that horse would be your responsibility. To feed, curry, ride. You think you're up to it, son?"

"Yes sir!" Ethan's glance bounced between Dixon, Drake and Frank. As suddenly as he'd inflated, Ethan deflated. "Mom hates horses. She's afraid of them. I don't think she'll let me do that."

"You let me worry about that." Frank nodded to the mudroom. "Go get your coat on. Remember your gloves. It's cold as hell out there."

Ethan bolted from the kitchen only to halt in the doorway and turn. "Grandpa Marshall, please don't tell Mom what I said. She'd be upset."

Dixon loved that Frank wanted Ethan to call him grandpa. It made his brother's transition into the Marshall clan almost seamless. There wasn't a dry eye in the house when Frank had told Ethan to call him that. Even Joy was blinking hard, and it took a lot to move his wife to an almost outward display of emotion.

Frank crossed his arms and rocked back on his heels before he grunted, "Won't. Don't see the need." Frank pointed to the mudroom and cocked his head. Ethan grinned and scrambled out of the room.

"You know, yesterday, when you gave every family a puppy, I think Ethan was a little upset he was excluded." Dixon put his hand on his father's shoulder. "But, seriously, you don't have to give him a horse."

"Well, as I explained to Ethan before I gave out that litter of golden retrievers, I had calculated one pup per family. Just because he surprised me, does not mean he doesn't deserve a present. He told me all about his wolf and assured me he didn't want another dog. Which is fortunate. I'm not sure that a wolf would take to a puppy. Although, for some reason, I know several sets of parents who are willing to donate a newly acquired puppy. Regardless, they have to suck it up. Kids need the responsibility of raising puppies." Frank crossed his arms, daring either he or Drake to say a word.

"Marcus and Royce are babies."

Dixon groaned, of course Drake went there.

"Jared and Christian can watch the dog until Marcus is old enough. Tippy is getting old. Having a puppy in the house will give that old dog new life, and Reece can handle two dogs. Stop picking at my Christmas gifts to my grandchildren or I'll give your wives a litter of barn cats. Each."

"You wouldn't." The cat Drake said he didn't like and wasn't his, but for whom he bought pricey canned food over in Hollister, was perched on a kitchen chair. All eyes went to the animal. Drake had found homes for each of her kittens and then had her fixed. From what Drake told him, Jillian wanted to keep all of the kittens.

"Drake, would you *please* shut the fuck up?" he begged his brother. He didn't think Joy would want kittens, but he hadn't thought she'd want Sasha, the dog-ette, either. The damn thing was permanently attached to Joy's ankle whenever she was home.

Ethan ran back into the kitchen, shoving his arms into the sleeves of his coat. His hat sat askew on his head and his gloves dangled from his free hand. "I'm ready. Will Talon and Reese be there?"

"This time is just for you boys. I'll take you up to the house after we see your new horse, and you can visit with the younger ones then."

He put his arm on Ethan's shoulder. "We'll have to think of a good name for your horse, so we need to get to know him or her. Spend some time with the foal and his momma."

Frank looked up at Dixon and Drake. "You two get a move on. I'm not waiting all day. Bring those gummy worms; I ran out of taffy."

CHAPTER 15

R yan sat on the couch and marveled at the symmetry in his life. He watched Bethanie talk and laugh with the host of women. She was happy here at the ranch but had confided to him last night she was ready to go home. Ethan, Talon, and Reece raced down the stairs, bundled up and ready to follow Frank out to the barn.

He felt her presence before he saw her.

"Absolute insanity," she muttered before she sat down.

"Absolute bliss," Ryan corrected. He was fucking happy. His wife and his son had an extended family now. Ethan, Reece and Talon were going to Skype with each other and, since the boys were on the East Coast, they'd already scheduled visits. Plus, Ethan's brothers had a standing invitation. Which meant more people knowing about the location of his home, but if it meant *his* family was happy, he'd wire

143

the mountain with so much security he'd know when a bird circled overhead. Whatever it took.

Joy stuck her hands on her hips and narrowed her eyes. "Who the fuck are you?"

Ryan shrugged. "A better version of the man I was. Who are you?"

"I'm a work in progress. Some days I don't recognize myself. Then I go away for work and I remind myself of who I actually am."

"You don't have to work." He'd walked away and look at the opportunity that presented itself. He was still astounded at the roller coaster ride his life had morphed into. He was hanging on for the entire ride because he had to know what was over the next hill and around the next bend.

"Yes, I do." Joy crossed her arms. "I'm not done. There is a reason I do what I do. I haven't reached a place in my life where I can walk away."

"Does your man agree with you working?" Ryan glanced at Bethanie. He would become a marionette for her. She pulled his strings and he happily and willingly danced to her direction.

"He would never give me an ultimatum. That isn't us. That isn't how we survive. Our relationship works for us." Joy plunked down on the couch, lifted her stocking clad feet underneath her, and curled up in the corner.

"I meant no disrespect to you or your husband. He's a good man. I'm happy for you. Not that you need my blessing."

"We've been friends for a long time Ryan. You are probably closer to me than anyone except Dixon. I'm glad you found your white picket fence." She snorted and chuckled.

"What?"

"This." Joy lifted a finger and made a circle indicating the hubbub of activity. "You, me, Asp, Anubis, Fury. Each one of us should be rotting in jail or dead."

"We made sacrifices for our country. We've fought hard to keep our world safe. Don't you think it is okay to forgive ourselves for our pasts and accept that maybe our beginnings don't comprise the totality of who we are?" He was damn certain he wasn't that person any longer and no matter how much she denied it, Moriah had changed, too.

Joy grunted. Which in Joy speak meant she'd take his words into consideration. He knew when to change the subject. "What's next for you?"

"We are going to Arizona. There is work the twins and Jillian need to complete. I love the desert. Most people think it is barren, but if you really look, it is beautiful in its own way."

Ryan smiled at her. "Like you, prickly on the outside, but soft under all the thorns."

Ethan came back in the house with Dixon and Drake. Joy's brow scrunched as she watched the men head their way. "Did you just call me a cactus?"

"It was a metaphor."

Joy swung her head to him. "What the fuck is a metaphor?"

"It's like a comparison." Ethan said.

"An analogy." Dixon added.

"Good one. A figurative expression." Drake high fived Ethan.

"Oh! An allegory or a parable!" Ethan raised his fist for Ryan to bump.

"Excellent, bud. It could also be called an adumbration." Ryan winked at him.

"Well, hell man, if you're going in the predictive sense, we can add prophecy, and foreshadowing." Drake shoved his hands in his coat pockets and smiled at Ethan.

"Prefiguration." Dixon added.

"Forecasting and prediction." Ethan added.

"Oh, for the love of my sanity, make it stop." Joy covered her ears and closed her eyes tight.

"Okay. Dad, it's nice out today, and we're going for a ride. Grandpa Marshall wants to know if you want to come with us. Say you will, please?" Ethan practically vibrated. "Reece and Talon's dads are coming. Dixon and Drake are coming. Joy, you can come too."

Ryan suppressed a laugh when Joy groaned. "Yeah, about that. I suddenly remembered I have to vacuum or some shit."

She popped off the couch and pulled Dixon to her, whispering in his ear. His face turned red and his eyes widened. Damn, he'd like to know what she said. He stood up and cleared his throat.

Joy sauntered away, the swish of her hips followed by her husband's eyes.

Dixon dropped his hand on Ethan's shoulder. "Hey, dude. I'll catch you after you come back in from the ride. I need to go help Joy... vacuum." Dixon smiled hugely at his brother's bark of laughter and followed Joy.

Ethan turned and gave him a disgusted look. "Dad, they aren't going to vacuum."

Ryan tried damn hard to keep a blank expression on his face. Thank God for years of training. "No, son, I don't think they are."

Ethan shook his head and offered his hand to Ryan. "Come on. They don't know what they're missing. There is nothing better than a ride."

Drake exploded into laughter, and Ethan turned and frowned at his brother. The man had his hands on his knees and tears in his eyes.

Ryan cuffed Ethan on the shoulder and shook his head. *Out of the mouths of babes.* "Let's go, bud. I'm sure Dixon will get a good ride in later."

Drake flopped onto the couch howling, his insanity pulling all eyes in their direction.

"You know, my brothers are kinda strange." Ethan sighed, shook his head, and led Ryan toward the kitchen where his coat, gloves, and hat hung on pegs.

Ryan tugged on Ethan's hand, stopping him as they passed Bethanie. He wrapped his arm around her and dropped a kiss on her lips. "We are going for a ride with the rest of the family."

She smiled wide. "Perfect. I'm going to help cook dinner and show Amanda pictures of my garden. She's really interested in the hydroponics option because the growing season here is so short." Bethanie dropped her eyes to Ethan. "Please be careful and listen to the men with more experience than you."

"I will. When we get back, you'll come out and visit my new colt, right? You promised. We still have to name him. I'm torn between Ranger and Rascal. He's feisty, so probably going to go with Rascal." Ethan narrowed his eyes at his mom. "You know he can't hurt you; he's a baby."

"No, I know. I most definitely will come see him. We need to get a bunch of pictures of him. Amanda said she'd ask Mr. Smith to take a picture every week so you can see how he is growing."

"Yeah, Grandpa said he'd grow up fast and that Mr. Smith was better with technology, so I gave him my email address." Ethan shoved his hands into his pockets and a huge smile spread across his face. "When you guys go on your honeymoon, I'll get to stay here. Grandpa Marshall said if Dixon and Drake have to go to Arizona while I'm here, he'd watch me."

"Oh, I..." Bethanie blinked at Ryan. He smiled at her and cocked his head.

"Come on, Mom, I'll be driving in a couple years. Plus, I don't want to go with you. All you're going to do is kiss and make out," Ethan scoffed.

"Yeah, Mom." Ryan mimicked.

"We'll talk about it. I still have a lot of questions."

Ethan lifted his fist to Ryan. "That wasn't a no."

"Score." Ryan bumped knuckles and then bent down and kissed his wife. "Thank you." He whispered just before he kissed her.

She smiled and winked. "Go, have fun. We'll be leaving soon, and he'll be cooped up in the truck for three days."

Ryan kissed her again and headed to the back door behind the bouncing ball of energy, also known as his son.

CHAPTER 16

Lycos shoved his hands in his parka and tucked his head as far as he could into the collar of his jacket. South Dakota had decided to turn into an Arctic wonderland. It was beautiful yesterday, for Christmas. Today, it was colder than a witch's tit in a brass bra buried in the frozen tundra of Alaska on the coldest day of the fucking year. Damn it his mountaintop got cold, but the wind in South Dakota seem to start somewhere in Idaho, gather speed over Wyoming and Montana, and slam into the state like a battering ram. *Fucking frigid.*

He quickened his pace as he approached the building where Anubis said to meet. This ranch was a cornucopia of surprises. It was going to take a couple weeks for him to adjust to the fact that Fury was actually alive. When he first saw the man at the house at dinner, he thought he had seen a ghost. It gave him hope, though. Hope that his own existence could carry on under the scope of most of humanity. Not being a blip on the screen was a good thing.

He entered the holding area of the small, unobtrusive building. The outside definitely gave no indication of what was inside. The holding area, however, gave everything away. Lycos noted the latest technology installed throughout the room. As the door shut behind him, he knew he'd never be able to exit without someone inside that facility allowing him to do so. He glanced up at the camera and sneered. Anubis wanted him here, well, he was here.

A distorted, disembodied voice cascaded from a speaker hidden somewhere in the room. "About fucking time you showed up."

Lycos chuckled. "Sue me. I'm on fucking vacation. I slept in."

The door clicked behind him. Lycos spun at the sound.

"Yeah, about that." Bengal opened the door and extended his hand into the hallway.

Lycos stood firm in the middle of the holding area. "Why do I have a feeling I'm not going to like what you're going to tell me."

"Nothing I say is going to alter what you have right now." Bengal met his eyes and Lycos knew his friend was speaking the truth.

Regardless, he stayed where he was. He crossed his arms over his chest. "Is that so?" Lycos heard the laugh before he saw the man.

Fury came into view. "You're keeping our boss waiting."

Lycos smiled and cocked his head. "Pretty fucking difficult to keep *your* boss waiting. You're dead, and last time I checked, I was no longer employed."

Fury lifted an eyebrow and growled, "Get your ass in here before I close this door and you miss an opportunity of a lifetime."

"Well, hell, who the fuck can ignore an invitation like that?" Lycos sauntered forward. To say he was curious would be short selling it. However, he couldn't go work as a Shadow. He would never spend months away from Ethan and Bethanie. On the mountaintop, his limited connection to the outside world restricted any opportunity Guardian could provide. Still, he was willing to listen. Any commitment would come after he talked to Bethanie. Not that he could share specifics, but what he could share, he would. Hell, he was already *considering* whatever opportunity Fury had waiting for him. He needed to halt that train in its tracks. He was out. It felt good, for the most part.

He followed Bengal and Fury down the hallway, through a secure door that would rival anything at Fort Knox. They descended at least thirty feet. An underground room? At the bottom of the stairs, Bengal opened another mammoth, reinforced, alarmed, door. As Bengal and Fury stepped through, Lycos whistled. What he thought was a room turned out to be an underground facility. "This is fucking sweet." His eyes searched the area. What he wouldn't give to see the plans for this place. Whoever laid it out and made it secure knew what the fuck they were doing. "Who the fuck designed this place?" Lycos spun slowly as he took in the complexity of the build.

Fury put his hands on his hips and cocked his head. "If I'm not mistaken that would be your stepsons?" He looked at Bengal. "Right?"

"Say what now?" Lycos snapped his head toward Fury.

"Dixon and Drake are stepbrothers to your adopted son. That makes his mother their stepmother. You married her. That makes them your stepsons." Fury glanced from one man to the other. "Right?"

"Holy fuck balls." Lycos scrubbed his face with his hand. "I could have lived my life perfectly content without ever knowing that." Those two grown ass men were his stepsons. How fucking weird was that? *Shit*. His stepson's wife had once been his lover. *Yeah, best not to go there.*

Bengal slapped him on the shoulder. "Come on, man, Gabriel is waiting."

Lycos followed the men down a long hallway into a conference room. Gabriel and Anubis sat at the head of the table. Fury and Bengal pulled out chairs sat down. Gabriel stood and extended his hand. "Thank you for coming to see me. I appreciate you taking time away from your family, especially now."

Lycos grasped the man's hand. He had met

Gabriel a couple times. Once, only in passing, at an event where Lycos was undercover. One time before that, they'd met when a mission went to hell in a handbasket. Gabriel drove Guardian. Were Lycos a fanciful man, he'd say Gabriel was Guardian's soul and perhaps the Kings, its heart. "Nobody actually told me I would be meeting you, sir. I would've been on time. Them? I don't give a shit if I make them wait."

"Thanks a lot, asshole." Anubis mumbled. The room erupted with laughter. Lycos sat when Gabriel took his seat.

"There have been some changes to the organization recently, the majority of which pertain only to that portion which remains visible. However, as we evolve and our missions change, the Shadows are going to take on more and more responsibility. I plan on integrating some of the Shadows with teams. We have psychological reports which indicate what Shadows should be able to perform with a team and those who would not." Gabriel shifted a folder from the middle of the table and pulled it toward him.

Lycos stared at Fury as Gabriel spoke. He couldn't quite figure out why both he and Fury were here, but he'd let the situation play out.

"Additionally, Demos has tapped out. He is no longer available to recruit our Shadows." Gabriel flipped open the folder and lifted a sheet of paper. Lycos leaned forward at that bit of information. Demos had rescued him—been his Guardian angel.

"We have built a complex in Arizona, the majority of which is destined to be similar to this ranch complex. It contains a small clinic that will remain relatively small, unlike the facility here. It also has enhanced training facilities and limited billeting. It will grow as needed. Fury has agreed to take on the responsibility of managing that complex. His wife, Dr. Ember King, has agreed to head up the medical facility." Gabriel laid the paper in his hand down and pushed it to the side. He picked up another sheet of paper from the file.

Lycos spun in his chair and eyed his former colleague. "You're confident there is no connection between your past and your present?"

Fury nodded. "The operative I was has long since been forgotten. Gabriel has kept close tabs on any loose ends who may have wanted Fury terminated. Life has a way of taking care of the refuse who may have known me. I'm confident enough to take my wife and child to Arizona."

Lycos absorbed that information as he returned his attention to Gabriel. The man waited until all eyes were upon him again before he continued.

"At the Arizona complex, Fury will continue to ensure our Shadow architects are trained so our deep covers are ironclad. Facilities are now complete to ensure all official documentation can be duplicated in-house, without compromise." He looked at Anubis. "The holographic machine was acquired?"

Anubis nodded. "Yes, sir. The Department of State

will never know."

Gabriel put the piece of paper he was holding on top of the other paper he had moved to the side. "That leaves the replacement for Demos." Gabriel caught Lycos in a direct gaze.

Realization of what was being asked of him slowly slithered down his spine. "I'm not qualified."

"Actually, you are exceptionally qualified." Gabriel lifted a piece of paper from that damn folder. "The construct of this position requires massive research. All information required on each candidate will be gathered and provided to you by our intelligence section. However, each candidate requires an individual assessment. You have the time, the intelligence, schooling, and experience, to know what kind of person would make a good Shadow. Psychiatric evaluations happen *after* a candidate has been vetted by you. If, at any time, the evaluations of the candidate and your determination of suitability are in conflict, your determination will win out and the candidate will not proceed."

Lycos leaned forward. "And by not proceed, you mean they are eliminated."

Gabriel set the piece of paper down. He steepled his fingers and stared at all of them as he spoke. "Each one of you were vetted through this process. Each one of you committed crimes against this nation and its people. Each one of you had redeeming qualities. None of you—" Gabriel held each man in a steady gaze for several seconds before he spoke again "—would have survived. Your only hope to remain alive was incarceration in the criminal justice system. It's more likely you would have died on the streets. Guardian saved each one of you from yourselves, and look at what you have now. You were once lost. Is there any doubt in anyone's mind that becoming a Shadow saved your lives?"

Fury leaned forward. "I murdered the man who killed my father. The new sheriff, who took over from my dad's old deputy, was tracking me down. He had uncovered evidence that my dad's replacement suppressed. I would have been convicted of murder. Mississippi has the death penalty. No doubt. Demos and Guardian were my salvation."

"Demos and Guardian took me from the streets moments before the FBI raided my home. My revenge against my father's enemies had put me on their scope." Anubis shrugged. "I was destined for death row for poisoning the Isadore crime family's elite."

Bengal looked at Lycos. "You know my story. You know what Gabriel said is true. Up on that mountain, you can sift through the volumes of information Guardian can push to you. You can narrow down the acceptable and eliminate the unacceptable. If you want, and if Gabriel will allow it, I will help you make the final call on the candidates. You don't need me. We both know you are a fucking genius. You need to consider this, Lycos. Be Guardian's contact with the people you evaluate as worthy. They will have a choice. Accept, or deal with the consequences of their crimes. All of us know that Demos saw us, truly saw us, for who and what we were. You have that capacity, Ryan. You can see the light in the darkness. We all recognize that ability in you. You were recommended for this position by me."

"And me." Anubis confirmed.

"You were my first choice." Fury added.

"The position is yours to accept or reject. Of course, on occasion, the job will take you off your mountain." Gabriel put all the papers back into the folder and shut the cover. "I'm sure you would like time to consider the ramifications and consequences of accepting a position of this nature."

Lycos leaned back in his chair. "Was Demos ever detected? Did he have a family?"

Gabriel chuckled. "His fifth grandchild is entering high school this year. He's decided his wife needs him at home full-time. She's not quite as sure he needs to be home as he is."

Anubis turned in his chair. "We have been monitoring your ripples. If there was any indication this assignment would place either you or Bethanie in danger, you would not have been approached." He looked to Gabriel for confirmation.

"I will not lie to you. At this point, recruitment for the Shadows is low risk. However, the people you will recruit are volatile, scared, and some are backed into a corner. Defending yourself may be a very real possibility. Your skills would need to remain sharp and current, and that means training and quarterly evaluations. As we normally only recruit one to three Shadows a year, the majority of your efforts would be going through the list of possible recruits."

Lycos leaned forward on his forearms and laced his fingers together as he stared at his wedding ring. "I appreciate the offer. I'll think about it and talk to Bethanie. Not about specifics, of course, but about the possible travel." He looked directly at Gabriel. "I'm not going to lie. If she agrees, I'm still going to hesitate to take this job. Demos was a lifesaver for many of us. I don't know that I could fill his shoes."

"I'm not asking you to fill his shoes, Lycos. I'm asking you to walk your own path. Demos selected carefully. I am certain your selections will be different. I expect the candidates you choose to have different attributes than those Demos looked for in the people he recruited. You have an advantage. You have walked as a Shadow, and you know what it takes to live in the darkness. Demos did not. He used his gut to make determinations on each of you. I'll need to know your decision by the New Year. I hope you'll take the assignment." Gabriel took the folder and stood up. "But whatever the decision, I thank you for what you have done not only for Guardian but for our nation." Gabriel extended his hand again.

Lycos stood and clasped the founder of Guardian Security's hand. He looked into Gabriel's eyes and knew in that moment he *was* going to accept. Yes, he'd talk to Bethanie, but if he could save one person from the ruinous trajectory his life had been on, then damn it, the safety concerns and travel off the mountain would be worth it.

Gabriel smiled and winked at Lycos before he spun and exited the room.

Lycos glanced at Fury. "Good luck in Arizona. I hope you didn't bite off more than you can chew."

"Well, if shit works out, I'll see you around, regularly." Fury rose and headed for the door. He tapped the door frame on his way out of the room. "And that, my friend, would be a good thing."

Anubis and Bengal stood, motioning toward the door. Lycos strolled out in front of them and looked down the hall. "So, what's the likelihood of Dixon and Drake showing me the plans for this facility?"

Anubis laughed and Bengal clamped a hand on his shoulder. "Dude, sign on to this job, and I'll guarantee Dixon and Drake will bore you to tears with the details of this facility."

He strolled toward the exit with two of the very few people who'd walked a mile in his shoes. The enticement of the building plans wasn't necessary, but he'd make sure Anubis remembered that comment. He never imagined he'd go back to work for Guardian. His life, previously filled with death and desolation, had been saved by his wife and son. Maybe, just maybe, he could impact another man or woman in a positive way so they had a chance at a life that mattered, and perhaps, a life that could be filled with love.

EPILOGUE

F rank Marshall sat on his front porch swing, a tumbler of his best scotch in his hand. The radiant heaters blasted away the still cold of the South Dakota evening and cloaked the porch in warmth. He pushed the swing back and let it creak to and fro. The peace of the evening was a shattering difference to earlier in the day. He'd watched as his King family boarded aircraft and left for the east coast. He'd been up at zero dark thirty to say goodbye to Ethan, Ryan and Bethanie. That boy was a miniature Dixon or Drake, and sharper than a wet-stone honed switchblade. His mom was a sweet woman, and from all accounts, his new father was a man who was up to raising a boy that intelligent.

The front door opened. He nodded a greeting and motioned to the other swing.

Gabriel leaned back heavily into the cushions. "It was good to see everyone again. It's been awhile."

"Glad you and Anna could drop by after having Christmas with your kids in New York. Sorry they couldn't make it this year. The crowd seemed smaller." Frank chuckled along with his friend. The crowd grew every year and he loved it.

"Gabbie had one day off before she had to travel for business. Time wouldn't allow us to get her to make her meeting if we came out here. Plus, the boys had to report back this morning. They were heading back to Tyndall Air Force Base. The little one? She's heading to Paris to study fashion design. This from a girl who wouldn't wear anything but jeans and t-shirts. Maybe next year." Gabriel paused and looked at the drink he carried. "I can't believe they are adults with careers. Seems like yesterday they were in diapers."

Frank grunted. "Had enough of those around here this year."

"Damn, see I know I should have brought Anna out sooner. She can't wait for grandchildren. I can." Gabriel chuckled and pushed the swing making it sway. "So, everyone made it home this year?"

"Yup." He sipped his whiskey. "They made an effort because of my health. I was happy to give 'em good news." He pointed at Gabriel. "I owe what's left of my life to you and your contacts."

Gabriel scowled and shook his head. "You'd have done the same thing for me."

"In a fucking heartbeat, my friend," he confirmed.

"You don't owe me shit. Besides, how many hours

have we sat in these swings and discussed Guardian? Who else can I trust to share my frustrations, aspirations, and hopes with?"

"Anna." Frank watched his friend almost choke on his drink.

After he caught his breath, he muttered, "Besides her, idiot."

"From what you've told me, you're going to have your hands full. Guardian will be growing and changing. It is a rite of passage for those who survive."

"Just like eating an elephant." Gabriel conceded.

"One bite at a time." Frank pushed his swing again. "How are you going to do it?"

"Small, precision strikes. Death by a thousand cuts. Compact, quicker teams that get in and get out. Faster, more streamlined, and easier to move and position. My prayer is the blood doesn't spill past those who need to be eliminated."

Frank nodded. He watched Gabriel stare into his tumbler. Unease radiated off him in waves.

"I'm taking Joseph to Arizona." Gabriel met his concerned stare. "He's clean. No one is tracking him. Those who know his identity as anything other than Joseph King know he'd skin them alive if they talked. I feel confident I can set him and his family up in Arizona and take care of them."

Frank grunted. He had no doubt Gabriel could take care of Joseph, but that was a moot point, because Joseph could and would take care of his family and himself. "What do you have him doing there?"

"He'll be heading up the facility. What he's learned here will be invaluable as we work on our deep cover profiles. Ember will be in charge of the hospital. We have the operations center for our people connected to the one here. Necessity dictates we separate the training facilities. People in Joseph's old profession will be run through his facility. Keeping everything segmented is safer for all people concerned."

"So, what happens to the huge facility you just buried in my back pasture?"

Gabriel chuckled. "Oh, believe me, we are going to use it. Arizona will be for the newer Shadows, the ones still learning the ropes. This facility is for our key operators, for developing missions and working the logistics with the key players instead of just inserting our assets into agendas we force on them."

"Trust but verify. Checks and balances." Frank nodded. He got it. Gabriel was playing his cards the way he would if it were up to him. If an enemy were to find a way into Guardian's ranks, a centralized location for all assets would make that complex a target.

"Indeed." Gabriel leaned forward. "Challenges await us. With the King family at the helm of Guardian, I'm free to concentrate on those burdens. I could use a confidential assistant. A man with experience, common sense, and who will call a pile of bullshit exactly what it is. Officially."

Frank cocked his head at Gabriel. "Officially, as in working for you?"

"No. Never. You'd work with me."

"What about your sons and daughters?"

"The boys aren't quite ready to assume that type of responsibility. The girls have no interest in Guardian."

"Huh." Interesting. This time, Gabriel didn't deny that those twin boys of his would play a role in the company. Usually, he said they were happy serving their country in the military.

"I assume that grunt meant yes."

"I won't leave my ranch." He was born on this soil. He'd die here.

"I wouldn't ask you to. I want Chief to outfit your office with the latest in tech. I want to be able to call you and use you as a filter and a sanity check. Jason, Jacob, Jared, and Jewell are spun up and running their divisions. Nic and Jade are doing remarkably well with the PSO division. Joseph has Arizona. Chief has the ranch. I have Kent Armstrong in Human Resources and damned if the man isn't a recruiting machine. The twins and Jillian are my foundational engineers, but I need someone who knows the direction I want my organization to go. Yeah, I have the wills and estate planning done, but Guardian is my baby. If I were to die tomorrow, nobody would know what my plans are or why I'm heading that direction. Mind you, I have no intention of dying. I have a clean bill of health, but for my *mental* health, I want a person I have absolute trust in to talk to, work things through with, and who will be a voice of reason. Absolute power corrupts absolutely and I am not immune. Besides, I *need* my friend, and you, my friend, fucking scared the shit out of me this year."

He nodded. He'd scared the shit out of everyone, including himself. "I'll do it, but not as a paid position. Keelee and Smith run the ranch. We have hands who do the heavy lifting. I'll be available for you; let you know when I won't be. I can't put Amanda at risk, or any of the grandchildren. My kids are well aware of the risks of their professions, so I'm not worried about them."

"That will work for me. Now, let's go inside before Anna and Amanda have us booked on some cruise around the world." Gabriel stood up and stretched.

"I wouldn't mind that too much. Except for the water."

"Sharks." Gabriel nodded.

"Hurricanes." Frank added.

"Pirates."

He stood and finished his drink. "Icebergs."

"We sound like the boys." Gabriel chuckled.

"Hell, man, I'm still a kid inside this old man's body. Walking by the mirror still shocks the hell out of me."

"Ain't that the truth." Gabriel chuckled and elbowed him before he headed into the house. "Too bad we can't show those young ones what we were like in our prime."

He grunted. No one would believe them. He headed toward the switch to kill the heaters. The light glow from the machines faded into darkness. He looked up at the multitude of stars in the heavens and smiled. He'd been granted a longer stay on this Earth. He remembered praying hard, bargaining with the Big Guy above, begging for more time. A fresh, healthy start was far better than he could have hoped for. He could make an impact, so he'd work hard at making this country and the world a better place for his children and their kids. After all, he was a Guardian. Again.

ABOUT THE AUTHOR

USA Today and Amazon Bestselling Author, Kris Michaels is the alter ego of a happily married wife and mother. She writes romance, usually with characters from military and law enforcement backgrounds.

Printed in Great Britain
by Amazon

48527499R00106